In the Duke's Arms

Carolyn Jewel

Jewel Books

Copyright

This book is a work of fiction. Names, characters, places, and incidents are the product of the author's imagination or are used fictitiously. Any resemblance to actual events, locales, or persons, living or dead, is coincidental.

Copyright © 2014 by Carolyn Jewel

All rights reserved. Except as permitted under the U.S. Copyright Act of 1976, no part of this publication may be reproduced, distributed, or transmitted in any form or by any means, or stored in a database or retrieval system, without the prior written permission of the publisher.

Cover Design by BookBeautiful.com

ISBN: 978-1-937823-35-1

cJewel Books

About In The Duke's Arms

He's made a horrible impression on the love of his life, but Christmas is a time for second chances.

The Duke of Oxthorpe has kept his heart under lock and key. Everything changed when he met Miss Edith Clay. His hopes for true love took a turn when Edith's rich cousin sought to attract his offer of marriage. But Oxthorpe is so smitten with the former poor relation that he goes through intermediaries to sell Edith a property as close as possible to his own.

Edith always saw the duke as haughty and arrogant. As Christmas approaches, Oxford reveals himself to be reserved, considerate, and—blame the mistletoe—an accomplished kisser! Edith has a choice: hold Oxthorpe's earlier behavior against him or embrace the altogether unexpected holiday gift.

Books By Carolyn Jewel

HISTORICAL ROMANCE SERIES

Sinclair Sisters Series
Lord Ruin, Book 1
A Notorious Ruin, Book 2

Reforming the Scoundrels Series
Not Wicked Enough, Book 1
Not Proper Enough, Book 2

Other Historical Romance
Scandal
Indiscreet
The Spare
Stolen Love
Passion's Song

Anthologies
Christmas in Duke Street
Dancing in The Duke's Arms
Christmas In The Duke's Arms
Midnight Scandals

Novellas
A Seduction in Winter
An Unsuitable Duchess
In The Duke's Arms
One Starlit Night
Moonlight A Regency-set short(ish) story

PARANORMAL ROMANCE

My Immortals Series
My Wicked Enemy, Book 1
My Forbidden Desire, RITA finalist, Paranormal Romance, Book 2
My Immortal Assassin, Book 3
My Dangerous Pleasure, Book 4
Free Fall, a novella
My Darkest Passion, Book 5
Dead Drop, Book 6
My Demon Warlord, Book 7

Other Paranormal Romance
Alphas Unleashed, Anthology *Dead Drop*
A Darker Crimson, Book 4 of *Crimson City*
DX, A *Crimson City* Novella

FANTASY ROMANCE

The King's Dragon – A short story

EROTIC ROMANCE

Whispers, Collection No. 1

Acknowledgments

My thanks go out to my agent, Kristin Nelson, for her unwavering support of my career. Carolyn Crane, thank you so much for your early and emergency reading. As ever thanks to my son Nathaniel and my sister Marguerite and my nephew and nieces, Dylan, Lexie, and Hannah. Also, thanks, Bella, for not eating any of my shoes. Recently.

Chapter One

The Duke's Arms, Hopewell-on-Lyft, Nottinghamshire, England, 1817

AWARENESS SHIVERED DOWN Oxthorpe's spine. He had no notion why but took the reaction as a sign he ought to pay attention. He braced one booted foot on the edge of the plank table and tipped back his chair until it rested on the wall behind him. He had no company at this table by the fire. It was a place reserved for him alone. A carved swan and griffin adorned the top of his chair.

That no one dared join him suited him. He preferred solitude even when in public. Especially in public. He sipped the dark ale the innkeeper brewed in his basement. As good or better than any produced by the larger brewer two towns over. Wattles, the proprietor of the coaching inn, supplied Killhope with a regular measure of this ale. The common room of The Duke's Arms was crowded with a mix of locals and travelers. The locals were closing out their day with dinner before heading home. Others awaited their connections to parts north or south. From his seat, he could see the inn's wooden sign with its painted swan and griffin echoing, rather loosely, those carved into his chair.

When he was not looking out the windows, his inelegant position gave him a view of his boot. The left of a decent pair of boots. Suitable for the country. He'd liked them well enough three years ago; the leather was supple even still. But these excellent boots did not have the folded top cuff of his new pair. Nor did they have a maroon tint to the leather, which he thought would set a fashion—if it were possible for a man like him to set a fashion for anything but striking fear into hearts.

He ought to be wearing his maroon top-boots and was not. Because he could not. The left of his new boots, never worn but for assuring the fit, had gone missing from Killhope. Servants had searched the house and grounds top to bottom and found nothing.

Just as he was about to conclude that nothing untoward was going to happen after all, the front door opened.

Winter air blasted through the room. Several of the patrons near the door shivered. A woman of about thirty came in. Oxthorpe straightened his chair and set his beer on the table. For the last month, he'd been telling himself he was prepared for this moment. He was not. This was inevitable, that they would at some point be in the same place. His heart banged away at his ribs.

She was dressed against the chill in a black woolen cloak, hood up so that one did not see the color of her hair and little of her face other than that she was pale complected. She was of medium height. Her eyes were brown, not that he could see that from here, but they were.

The maid closed the door behind them and stood to one side, hands clasped and head down. Of this he approved, both that her maid held her employer in the proper respect and that she'd brought a servant with her.

With one hand, because she held a paper-wrapped parcel in the other, the woman pushed back the hood of her cloak. A spray of tiny blue flowers adorned her brown hair. She had hair combs, too. Ebony, if he was not mistaken. This was an embellishment he had never seen from her in Town. "Good afternoon, Mr. Wattles."

Miss Edith Clay brightened the room with her presence. Just from walking through the door, she'd made the room a happier place. This was true despite his having spent the last several months assuring himself his recollection of her had to be incorrect.

His recollection was not incorrect. It was appallingly accurate.

Wattles grinned from behind the bar where he stood to pull beer or ale from the tap and tell stories or, often, listen to them. "Delightful to see you, miss."

Mrs. Wattles, who had emerged from the kitchen for a word with her husband, saw Miss Clay and headed toward her. She wiped her hands on her apron and folded them beneath the fabric. "Always a pleasure to see you, Miss Clay."

"Thank you, Mrs. Wattles." Her smile hollowed out his chest. She'd changed since last he saw her. She was brighter. More vibrant. Happiness suited her. "You are so kind."

The Wattleses' daughter, Peg, came into the common room from the back carrying an empty tray, heading, he presumed, to the kitchen.

"You're early to pick up your dinner, miss," Mrs. Wattles said.

Peg stopped to curtsy. "Good day, miss."

"Peg. I hope you're well." She tugged at the wrist of one of her gloves. Blue kid.

Her focus returned to Mrs. Wattles, and while she was so engaged, Oxthorpe took the opportunity to study her and tightly wrap up his response to her. He had a clear view of her from where he sat. To see him, however, she would have had to look in the shadows at the rear of the room, and she had not done so. Why would she? She'd not come to see him. For one thing, his visit this afternoon had not been scheduled.

Waning afternoon light shone through the windows to the courtyard, with its glimpse of the Great Northern Road. A groom hurried toward the stables at the rear, his arms wrapped around his middle. Her maid was not a Hopewell-on-Lyft local. He supposed she must be from London.

"Yes, I am a little early picking up my dinner," Edith said. "But that's not why I've come. Not the only reason, that is."

Strange, seeing her without her younger and prettier cousin. In London last year, and later in Tunbridge Wells, he'd got used to seeing them together. Inseparable those two, even though Miss Clay was the elder by a decade. Two years younger than he. Unlike him, she was cheerful. Always pleasant. So bloody, horribly happy even though she had no particular looks, and at the time he met her, no fortune whatever. She had been, in fact, entirely dependent on her relations.

Mrs. Wattles waved to her daughter. "Tell them Miss Clay is here to pick up her supper."

"Yes, Mum."

"Thank you, Mrs. Wattles." She glanced around the room, but her gaze slid over him. Even in London, always happy. "How is your father, ma'am? Better, I hope."

Mrs. Wattles's father was ninety years old and, lately, in failing health. "As well as can be expected, I think. He says thank you for the bread and broth you sent."

"I shall send more, if it would be welcome."

"He would enjoy that, miss." Wattles bent a knee. "We'd be grateful if you did."

She adjusted the parcel in her arms. The light through the windows turned her hair shades of walnut. "I hope you'll let me know if there is anything else you need."

"Thank you, miss."

By no stretch of imagination was Edith Clay anything but a pleasant-looking woman. Not unattractive. But nothing to make a man's head turn. She wasn't young. At twenty-seven, nearly twenty-eight now, thirty was not far off for her. A woman, not a girl. Her cloak separated to reveal a portion of a blue frock. Robin's-egg blue. That was unusual, her wearing colors. She never had before.

"I am here on account of a mystery most deep, Mrs. Wattles."

One of the laborers in the far corner of the main room came forward with a chair. The man set it down near where Miss Clay stood near the bow windows with her parcel in her arms, then backed away. Another of them pushed forward a chair for her maid. Her maid sent a grateful glance in the direction of the men.

"Thank you," Edith said.

He did not understand this fey power of hers to make people like her. He wondered if she'd walked here. If she had, she'd have a mile and a half through the cold when she left, and uphill, too. There might be snow this time of year. Likely so with the way the sky looked.

Edith perched on the edge of her chair, knees pressed together, feet aligned. She'd sat just so before, a woman of no importance, whom no one noticed when she was quiet. "I hope you can assist me."

Mrs. Wattles clasped her hands underneath her apron. "Whatever we can do."

She settled her parcel on her lap. "Did you know, Mrs. Wattles, that when I moved into Hope Springs, I found a note pinned to the wall in the entryway? Just above a crate. I thought it odd."

These were now more words than ever he'd heard her say at one time. In London, she had guarded every word against her cousin Clay's disapproval. There were more differences between the woman she'd been then and what she was now. Besides the fashionable clothes, her face was more animated, and though she was not a beauty, there was something there. She seemed freer now than she had been. Who would not be who had made a similar escape?

"What did the note say?"

"It was left, I presume, by the previous inhabitant, by way of instruction. It said, 'For Items Found.' Is that not peculiar? I thought it peculiar." She had a good, strong voice. She smiled with her voice, too. This, he thought, was the magic that had drawn him to her.

"What did you find?"

"Ah." She held up her gloved index finger. "I suspected as much. There have been things found at my home before."

"There might have been." Mrs. Wattles laughed.

She unwrapped the parcel she held. Several of the laborers and many of the travelers in the front room craned their necks to see. "When I returned from my morning perambulations to the vale and back, I found this in my driveway." She held up a boot. A gentleman's gleaming boot of maroon leather with a folded-down cuff. "Is this not most mysterious? I have not been in Hopewell-on-Lyft very long, so perhaps it is common, but it seems uncommon to me."

True. She'd been here a month, no longer.

"Perhaps one frequently finds a boot in one's drive." She was laughing at herself, delighted with the absurdity. So were the others. He, too, was smiling. Even though it was his boot.

Peg had returned from the kitchen, and she eagerly explained. "It's Mr. Paling's collie, miss. From Killhope." Paling being his groundskeeper. The man had a three-legged collie who followed him everywhere.

Edith tilted her head. Wide-eyed innocence played to perfection. "Are you certain? For this seems so very much like a boot, to me. It's not at all collie-shaped."

Mrs. Wattles laughed. Edith hadn't a mean bone in her body. Not one. She meant to amuse, and she did. He was amused, though he did not want to be.

"Mr. Paling's collie is excitable," Mr. Wattles said. He'd refilled someone's beer and now held it in one hand. "When she's in such a state, why she'll snatch up something near and dash away with it. She leaves it wherever she is when the passion wears off."

"Ah."

"When he comes here with the dog, we are careful to put away anything she might carry away with her." Wattles pushed the beer to the man waiting for it. "You're not so far from Killhope, miss. It's bound to happen."

"This is the duke's boot?"

Mrs. Wattles glanced over her shoulder at him. So did her husband. And Peg. And several of the locals. "I can't say if it is or it isn't."

Edith did not notice the stares in his direction because she was examining his boot. "Well. Not a princely boot, then, but a noble one. Yes, I see that now." With a sigh, she rewrapped his boot and retied the string. "I do wish I'd guessed that before I walked in the opposite direction from Killhope Castle."

Oxthorpe stood. He could do nothing else.

Her hands stilled, and her smile faded away. She stood and dropped into a curtsy. What did one say in such situations, when one knew a lady disapproved? "Miss Clay," he said.

"Duke." She'd given the field laborer a happier smile than she gave him. Most everyone else had stopped smiling, too. This was the effect he had on others. He was the Duke of Oxthorpe, and though he did his duty by his title and his estate, he was not beloved. He did not know how to be beloved the way Miss Clay was.

"You have my boot."

She turned her head to one side. To avoid meeting his gaze. "Do I? Your Grace."

"I'll try it on and let you judge the fit."

"That will not be necessary."

"It is when you doubt that it is mine." He walked to her, and she handed over his boot. He examined it when he'd sat on a chair Wattles brought for him. He would not have gone through with his ridiculous challenge to her except she thought he would not.

At last, she looked at him. Without warmth. "It isn't the collie's fault."

He drew off his boot with less effort than he'd expected and put on the other. A perfect fit. "There are tooth marks." Too late, he understood he'd spoken gruffly. Possibly, she thought he accused her of damaging his boot.

Her expression smoothed out, and then she did what she would never have done before. She smiled brightly and said, "I assure you, sir, they are not mine."

This was amusing. He recognized that. Several people guffawed, and he heard others trying not to laugh. Without allowing his annoyance and dismay to show, he changed boots again. "You relieve me, Miss Clay."

Once again, he had offended her. He should not care. He did not care. Why ought he to care about a woman like her? Except he did. He bowed, jaw clenched against the possibility that he would say more to offend. He strode out of The Duke's Arms with his bloody damned boot.

Chapter Two

EDITH FLICKED UP her hood against the crosswind. The air smelled like snow and felt like ice, and she hoped to make it home before either made her walk exceedingly unpleasant. She now regretted her decision to walk to The Duke's Arms with the no-longer-mysterious boot. She and her maid would be thoroughly frozen by the time they arrived home.

She walked faster, her maid keeping pace. Behind them came the thud of hooves on cold dirt and the creak and rumble of a carriage. Not the mail traveling south. She'd have heard the commotion of that.

She moved to the edge of the road. Her maid did the same. The carriage slowed, passed her, then stopped a few yards ahead. Her heart sank. Even without a coat of arms, this could only be the duke's carriage. No one else in Hopewell-on-Lyft could possibly drive so fine a vehicle, and besides, the groom clinging to the back wore the duke's livery.

The groom jumped down and ran to hold the head of the lead horse. The animals, four matched chestnuts, were fine enough that even she took a breath at their quality. Horses like that must cost hundreds of pounds.

The carriage window lowered and Ryals Fletcher, Duke of Oxthorpe, stuck his head out.

Wind blew his hair into disarray. Even so, he was grand and somber and terrifying. Not yet thirty. As if age mattered at all. Despite his relative youth, he frightened everyone with his stern face and eyes that looked at one with a thousand years of wealth and privilege. "Miss Clay."

She walked to the door so she would not have to shout a reply to his summons. She curtsied and said, "Your Grace."

"It is cold."

"It is winter." She reminded herself he was a duke, a man of significant wealth and responsibilities. She reminded herself that he had courted Louisa and stood poised to break her Louisa's heart or make her the happiest woman in England. There was yet hope for the match. Her cousin, Mr. Clay, had invited him to Holmrook for Christmas and, as yet, he had not declined.

He pushed open the door, and his groom jumped forward to hold the door and put down the step. "I shall see you home."

She might have refused, except that her maid shivered, and indeed, she, too, felt the bite of the wind despite her thick cloak. Fifteen minutes with the man would not kill her. "Thank you."

The duke stepped down. Impeccable clothing. Beautifully cut and worn on a frame that hinted, no, shouted, at physical strength. This had surprised her when she'd first seen him in London, that he looked like a man who controlled his body as harshly as everything else. She did not care for tall men.

"Your maid, too," he said. A laugh rasped along his throat, a growl from a man who appeared to have never laughed in all his days until now. From the side of her eye, she saw the groom look away. "No one will say I ravished two women."

My God. Was there anyone less gracious? Of course, if one was the Duke of Oxthorpe, who owned the better part of the land here and around Hopewell-on-Lyft and, indeed, the parish, one need not be gracious. He knew his place, and it was above everyone else. Far above.

He signaled to the groom with a motion that included her maid. "Keep that safe for Miss Clay."

With a grim expression, the groom took the dinner Mrs. Wattles had wrapped up for her. This being the cook's night off, Edith had fallen into the habit of taking away dinner from The Duke's Arms. The Wattleses were excellent innkeepers, and the kitchen at The Duke's Arms did a brisk trade for locals as well as travelers.

The duke extended his hand to her, and only then did it occur to her that he might be distinguishing her because of Louisa. He was not a man to make decisions in haste, that much she knew. She put her hand on Oxthorpe's and got in. His fingers closed around hers, and she felt the strength in him. She found it unpleasant, this awareness that he was so much stronger and larger than she. Her maid came in after.

The duke took the rear-facing seat. Could such a joyless man really be not even thirty? He ought to be a century old at least. And yet he had succeeded in winning Louisa's heart.

"Thank you," she said when he'd settled himself. He'd left his hat on their side, and she handed it to him. Beaver, with grosgrain ribbon around the base.

He set the hat beside him. The carriage started up. Edith smiled, got no reaction for her trouble, and settled on a study of the interior. As good an excuse as any not to look at him. Lacquered wood, black leather seats, gilt lanterns, and everywhere some echo of his coat of arms; a swan or a griffin carved or painted or worked in metal.

In these quarters, alas, it was impossible to behave as if she did not know he was there. Besides, it was rude, and like him or not, she did not wish to be rude to anyone, particularly not a man who oozed rank from every particle of his being, from his clothes, to his carriage, to the sapphire in his neckcloth.

He was handsome, and this was a circumstance that had surprised her in London, and again in Tunbridge Wells, and yet again in The Duke's Arms. Now, too. Handsome, yes, in an austere and condescending way, with a narrow face and sharp cheeks and his shockingly intense eyes. Even with his thick, dark hair mussed by the wind, he was frightening to behold.

She tried another smile, and again—nothing in return. No doubt he thought of her as little more than a servant, for her cousin Clay had treated her as if she were nothing more than that—without the need to pay her wages. Her parents had been in such financial straits when she was a child that they had been obliged, and grateful, to send her to live with her father's cousin.

Having done her best to be polite to the man, she contented herself with staring at her lap or at his hat on the seat beside him. She imagined him wandering the corridors of Killhope with no friends to keep him company, no callers not there on business, no one but his staff in the lonely, empty, dreary rooms. Killhope Castle was aptly named, for she saw no hope of anyone there ever smiling.

She stared out the window for some minutes then made the mistake of glancing out the other side. Her gaze collided with the duke's. His eyes were a clear, pale green. Why was he staring so intently when there was hardly another woman less interesting than she?

She smiled again.

He did not.

How awkward this was. Never had she met a man less careful of his impact on others. She frowned. Not that, not uncaring; oblivious. This puzzle distracted her from the dreadful silence. During her time in London, she had observed many a gentleman, more than a few of noble descent, and they had all been pleasant to her cousin, some more so than others, depending on their hopes for Louisa.

The duke, while never directly offensive to her, had not been an easy man to be around. Even in company, his silence soon went from unpleasant to oppressive. She knew she was not the only one to feel that way. She knew Louisa had overcome the man's silence. With her own eyes, she had seen him be charming to Louisa.

Once again, she caught his gaze without intending to. Thank goodness she had no reason to feel Louisa's despair of him. "I expect there will be snow tonight."

"Yes."

During those interminable years in her cousin's household, she had perfected a cheerful smile, and she gave him one now.

The duke leaned forward, a palm propped on his knee. "What fool walks out on a day like this?"

She'd spent so many years being agreeable because she must that she instinctively bent her head. But why, she thought as she did, ought she say nothing to such a statement? Why, when she was beholden to no one, ought she be silent? She lifted her chin. "It is a mile and a half from my home to The Duke's Arms. A walk of thirty minutes if I dawdle."

"Uphill."

"On my return, yes."

"You should have driven into town."

She folded her hands on her lap and kept to herself the fact that she did not yet possess a carriage. A wagon, yes, but not a carriage. Any moment they would be at her home, and she would be quit of this unpleasant man. She did not say another word until they arrived at Hope Springs. Her good mood returned in force. This was her home. Hers alone. The deed had her name on it, and when she went inside, everything would be hers and arranged to her taste.

The groom came around and opened the door. As she brought up the hood of her cloak again, the duke stepped out and stood beside the door, his hand extended to her. She let her maid out first and then descended herself, fingertips on his gloved hand.

As she curtsied to him, a snowflake drifted between them. She hated that he was right about the weather, not that it would have killed her to walk home with a few snowflakes in her hair. "Thank you. You were kind to convey me home in this weather."

He nodded.

Why wasn't he getting back in his carriage? She curtsied to him again. "Good day, Your Grace."

His eyes were as cold as the snowflakes in his hair, for he'd left his hat in the carriage. "I shall escort you to your door."

Every word he uttered was a command. Gruff, with no kind intent at all, and she, even with her new circumstances, had no choice but to endure. "Thank you."

Halfway to her door, the duke put out his elbow, and there was no remedy for this new awkwardness except for her to loop her hand through his arm. She was warmer at all the places where their bodies were close. Her front door was a mile away. Ten miles. A thousand. Could he not walk faster?

"You put in slate."

"I beg your pardon?"

He nodded at the paving stones. "Slate."

Her maid had already gone around to the back with their supper. "I did not wish to walk in the mud when the weather is damp."

"I approve." What haughty words. Good heavens. What if he'd not approved? What if he believed slate was the very worst material for her to have installed? Would he have expected her to remove it and replace it with something more to his liking? Likely, he would have. Likely, some of his neighbors would comply with such an expectation. Cousin Clay would have.

"Thank you."

"You are welcome."

Now he sounded as if he thought she'd hurry to her desk to write letters in which she informed her friends and acquaintances that the Duke of Oxthorpe had approved of her slate. She sneaked a look at him. He probably did think that.

At last, they reached the top stair where she put a hand on the door and bent a knee to him. "Thank you, Your Grace."

He gazed at her with his disconcerting eyes, and just as she was about to go inside without any resolution to their awkwardness, he said, "I never saw you wear that color before."

She glanced down at her blue dress. What a singular thing for him to notice. "It is a new frock."

Snowflakes melted in his hair. "Do you miss your cousin?"

Well, then. This was a development. Was all this awkwardness between them because of Louisa? "Do you mean Louisa?"

"I doubt you miss Mr. Clay."

"I do not." For Louisa's sake, she smiled. "I'd begun to wonder if you'd forgotten Louisa."

"No."

This was a most excellent development. He *did* feel something for Louisa. He did. "Louisa and my Cousin Clay are memorable, I'm sure you'll agree."

"What of you?"

She cocked her head, wondering what he meant by the odd inflection of his question. "Me?" She waved a hand. "I am the least memorable woman you'll ever meet."

"I disagree." His eyes bored into her. "I have never forgotten you."

Chapter Three

AT TWENTY PAST two, Edith knocked on the door of the Thomases' home on the eastern side of Hopewell-on-Lyft. She'd not meant to be late for this meeting, for this was not a social call, but the walk to the other side of the town had taken longer than she'd anticipated.

A wagon and two strong drays had been a necessary purchase for her move to Nottinghamshire. She had known at the time of her preparations for removal to Hope Springs that she would need a vehicle for her personal use. She'd continued to put off the purchase because every time she reviewed her budget and expenses, the cost of a carriage and suitable horse paralyzed her. Her father had spent unwisely, and that had ended with her sent to live with her cousin Clay.

The example of her father had taught her that while a single unwise purchase might cause no significant damage, a series of them would. Spendthrift choices multiplied. Her move to Hope Springs had come with unanticipated expenses. More furniture needed than she'd thought. Rooms that needed more than new paint. Fabric for curtains that she would not come to despise. A chimney to repair, a new hearth for the kitchen, half the buttery to be rebuilt once she'd bought cows and a bull. Chickens, too, and geese. There were gardens and lawns to manage. A flagstone path from the drive to the house. Servants to pay.

A carriage and associated expenses seemed intolerable when she could walk. No decision meant no change in her present finances. Every penny spent outside her allotted budget brought the specter of ruin closer. And so, despite the inconvenience, despite knowing she ought to have a carriage of some sort, she did not decide what to buy and continued to walk. Next quarter, she would make the purchase. Or the one after.

"Good day, miss." The Thomases' butler took her mantle, her muff, and her hat.

"Good day to you, too." She felt the difference between her being Miss Clay, dependent relative of Mr. Clay, and being Miss Edith Clay, a lady in possession of a fortune. She'd been invited for herself, and here she was, in pale pink muslin and silk, with a cashmere shawl around her shoulders.

"This way, miss. They are waiting for you."

In the parlor, she was not received as the least significant of the Clays, nor expected to behave as if she were. These women were waiting for her, not her relations. She'd been invited to join the committee that organized and raised funds for the quarterly assemblies. She had been flattered and thrilled to accept. The Christmas assembly was the largest such affair of the year, with residents from all ranks included in the celebration. The women here would, she hoped, become lifelong friends. Already, she knew she liked Mrs. Thomas exceedingly.

Mrs. Thomas met Edith halfway across the room. The older woman kissed her cheek. "Welcome, welcome. You know the others. Mrs. Anders, Mrs. Pembleton, Mrs. Herbert, and Mrs. Quinn. Mrs. Carrington was unable to attend today but sends her regards."

"Good morning, ladies." She curtsied. "I could not be more delighted to be here."

"My dear Miss Clay, do sit. We have an excellent tea." Mrs. Thomas escorted her to the table where the others were gathered. Edith made a mental note of the food and drink and the setting. One day, their meeting would be hosted at Hope Springs. She intended to make a good impression when her turn came.

"Thank you. So many delightful treats, Mrs. Thomas." Cheese, bread, meats, an array of pastries, cakes, and biscuits. Mrs. Quinn, a woman of Edith's age, poured her tea. "Thank you, ma'am."

"You're quite welcome."

Edith found herself presented with full privileges to choose whatever she preferred. Neither her cousin nor his wife would later take her aside and tell her how impolite it was for a lady of her station to take anything but the smallest, least interesting selections.

While Edith was busy serving herself, Mrs. Pembleton produced a slim notebook, which she opened. "This last public assembly of the year is, as you know, to be held Monday, December the twenty-second at the parish hall in Hopewell-on-Lyft." She looked around the table. "It is agreed we shall relocate to Carrington Close should there be a recurrence of last year's incident with the roof."

"Have we written to Mrs. Carrington to express our gratitude?"

"Yes. Done last week. Now, due to generous donations from His Grace and from Miss Clay—"

Polite clapping followed that announcement, which Edith acknowledged with a nod. Her donation to the committee had been a good use of a portion of the monies she allotted for charity.

"—our budget for the Christmas assembly is flush with funds. Extra decorations have been ordered and a wider selection of refreshments added to the menu." She glanced around the table. "We do need additional servants. If each of you would lend two healthy footmen for the day before, the day of, and the day after, I daresay we shall be competently staffed." She frowned. "Two footmen and two maids if we are at Carrington Close."

"Yes, yes," Mrs. Thomas said.

"His Grace has once again offered the use of his kitchen staff. I have written to thank him for that generosity."

Edith added to the clapping. When Mrs. Pembleton completed her report on the committee's efforts so far, she lifted a hand.

"You have the floor, Miss Clay."

"Hope Springs contains several acres of oak forest. May I offer to collect mistletoe from these trees? If there is a supply of ribbon, lace, or other notions from the decorations obtained for our purpose, I can provide all the bouquets of mistletoe we might wish to have at the assembly. After sending round a suitable sample for approval, of course."

"An excellent suggestion. Thank you, Miss Clay." Mrs. Pembleton made a note. "I shall send you such samples as might be useful for your exemplar."

Mrs. Pembleton folded her arms on the table and put her weight on them. "I am determined that *this* year we shall persuade His Grace to attend the Christmas assembly. All our hopes for a Christmas miracle rest upon you, Mrs. Thomas."

"I make no guarantees of a miracle."

Edith took in the various reactions to that. No one seemed astonished by the request. "Does he never make an appearance?"

"Not since 1810," said Mrs. Anders. "Before your time, Mrs. Quinn. And yours, Mrs. Thomas."

"Has he stayed away every year?" Edith kept her opinion of the duke's deliberate absence to herself, but truly, this was not well done of him.

"He prefers to stay locked away upon that hill," Mrs. Anders replied.

Edith's admittedly unfounded notion that His Grace the duke lived in dungeon-like conditions cemented itself in her head. She imagined him treading lonely passageways, a candle barely able to penetrate the dark, and all about him a dank and dampish smell. "He is a man driven by duty," Edith said. "Perhaps we might see success if we remind him of his responsibility to let the people of Hopewell-on-Lyft see him at our assembly."

"An excellent strategy, Miss Clay," Mrs. Thomas said.

She hid a pleased smile behind a sip of tea.

"It's never worked in the past." Mrs. Herbert added more sugar to her tea. "Even my poor dear Ernest, who would have been heir to the Earl of Hillforth were it not for Carbury, could never persuade him. I do think he should emulate the condescension of his neighbors of the better sort."

Edith decided then and there that Mrs. Herbert, a recent widow, was not destined to be a friend.

Mrs. Thomas let out a long sigh. "He ought to make an appearance, I agree. And Miss Clay is correct that one's best hope of convincing him to do anything is an appeal to duty. However, Tuesday last, Mr. Thomas and I dined with the duke, and when I asked if he would attend this year, he replied that he would not be at Killhope."

"Such a pity," Mrs. Anders said, "that he did not return here with a bride when he was in London last Season. We had such high hopes for him." She turned to Edith. "You do not know Oxthorpe—"

"Oh, but—"

"We were all of us convinced he would be married by now," said Mrs. Quinn.

"If only he'd found his duchess while he was away," Mrs. Thomas said. "*She* would surely convince him that to appear at our Christmas assembly must take precedence over most any other duty."

Mrs. Pembleton made additional notes while she spoke. "At least there is yet hope for those of you with daughters."

Mrs. Thomas shook her head. "As delightful and beautiful as are the young ladies of Hopewell-on-Lyft, I think it doubtful Oxthorpe will marry locally. If he meant to, he would have done so by now."

"A duke," said Mrs. Herbert with a delicate sniff, "must marry from the highest ranks of society. To marry for love would be a serious dereliction of duty, and as Miss Clay has been kind enough to remind us, our duke puts duty above all else. No, Oxthorpe must make a marriage of politics, or one that cements his fortune. There can be no other criteria. Do not imagine that he would marry for love."

"If we but knew what happened in London," Mrs. Quinn said after a moment's silence. "Did he meet any suitable young lady when he was there? Might he have fallen in love with a woman who spurned him?"

"Good heavens," said Mrs. Anders. "What young woman in her right mind would refuse a duke?"

"It happens," Edith said, "that I was introduced to him when he was in London." She found she rather liked the astonishment this produced. She answered questions as they came at her. Where had they met? Who had introduced them? Had they spoken often? Had the duke singled out any young lady? "My cousin, Mr. Clay, is an acquaintance of a gentleman who is a relation of an uncle of the present Viscount deVere. The duke attended a fete given by Lord deVere, which we also attended." She waved a hand. "Our introduction to him was made there." She looked around the table. "The duke was quite taken with my young cousin, Miss Louisa Clay."

Mrs. Herbert reached for a cake and placed it daintily on her plate. "Did he frighten all the other suitable young ladies?"

Edith glanced around the table. These were women she hoped would become friends, but she would not speak ill of the duke. "It's true he is a man of few words, but when he was in London, he was as charming as any other gentleman of like reserve might be. I mean to say, more charming than one might expect of him. There were times, I vow, when I was glad he was silent, for some gentlemen never are."

"Quite true," Mrs. Thomas said. "For all his solitary ways, our duke is a man of parts."

"He is." She laid a hand on the table. How odd. She felt protective of him. He *had* driven her home. Regardless of how awkward that had been, he'd not left her to walk home in the cold. "It was thought by many that he would offer for my cousin, Louisa. She is accomplished and attractive, and as gracious as one can imagine. You never in your life met a more agreeable young lady than she."

"Did he distinguish her?" Mrs. Quinn asked.

"He did."

"How often did he call on her? If he did." Mrs. Quinn leaned toward her, eyes wide. "Did he?"

"Three or four times at least in London. That many times in Tunbridge Wells and again when we were back in Town." On every one of his calls, Edith had sat in the parlor with Louisa and the duke, or walked with them in the garden, doing her best to keep the conversation going when Louisa flagged in the face of his silence.

"Tunbridge Wells, you say?"

"Yes, Mrs. Quinn. This past March, we went to Tunbridge Wells, and who should appear at the same hotel? His Grace."

The ladies of the committee exchanged significant looks.

"He danced with Louisa three evenings in succession."

"One wonders," said Mrs. Pembleton, "why he did not make her a proposal."

Edith would never forget Louisa's despair of the duke, nor that her father had pressured his daughter to bring the match around. As if Louisa could have done so by being constantly reminded of it. "An offer was expected, and not just by my cousin, Mr. Clay." She lifted her hands. "The duke, as you have all observed, is a singularly reticent man."

"Dour," said Mrs. Anders. "A dour man."

"No. No, not dour." But in that she must relent. Mrs. Anders was correct. "Perhaps a little, but His Grace is a man who does nothing without great and long reflection. He went to Tunbridge Wells, after all, and he did greatly distinguish her there."

"If he loves her," said Mrs. Quinn, "he will see her again. He must."

"Love." Mrs. Herbert raised her delicate brows. "I tell you, love will have nothing to do with his marriage when he makes it."

"Nothing else will do but for him to put everything in motion for his bringing home a bride," Mrs. Quinn said.

"Where did you say your cousin lives?" Mrs. Thomas asked.

"Northumberland. Near Holmrook."

"If it is true," said Mrs. Herbert, "and I doubt very much that it is, he ought not have delayed in bringing the matter to a conclusion. He risks a great deal by waiting to declare himself."

Mrs. Quinn set her chin on her palm and sighed. "A young lady might wait some time for the sake of a handsome duke."

"Does anyone know if he's called on the vicar recently?" Mrs. Anders asked. "That would tell us if we are on the right path, here."

"Oh," said Mrs. Pembleton. "Oh my. I hadn't realized."

"What is it?"

Mrs. Pembleton looked at each of the women in turn. "Yesterday I called on Mr. Amblewise, and he mentioned the duke had just left."

"This is wonderful news. Wonderful. So encouraging." Mrs. Thomas clasped her hands. "He told us, Mr. Thomas and me, that he expected to be at a property of his at the time of our assembly." She gave them all a significant look. "A property of his in Northumberland."

"Your cousin lives in Holmrook, did you say, Miss Clay?"

"Yes."

Mrs. Pembleton lifted a hand. "In Northumberland."

"That means nothing," said Mrs. Herbert.

"I do know," Edith said, "that my cousin has invited the duke to visit them."

"He's called on the vicar. He will not be at Killhope for the holidays. What else could it be except that our duke is in love?" Mrs. Quinn rested a hand over her heart. "Ladies, here is our Christmas miracle."

Chapter Four

WHEN EDITH LEFT the Thomases after the meeting, the weather was clear, and her spirits were considerably buoyed by such strong evidence that the duke was more serious about Louisa than she'd thought. He'd been invited to Holmrook for Christmas. He had told Mrs. Thomas he would not be at Killhope at the time of the assembly. He'd called on the vicar, Mr. Amblewise, only a few days in advance of when he would need to leave for Northumberland to make Louisa an offer of marriage.

By the time she reached the eastern outskirts of town, though she remained delighted about the duke and Louisa, the cold was now foremost in her thoughts. The wind had come up, and clouds obliterated any sign of blue skies. With the weather deteriorating like this, she would be a block of ice by the time she was home. She pushed her hands deep into her ermine muff and increased her pace. If she walked quickly, she could be home in under an hour.

She crossed the bridge over the Lyft and headed into the heart of town. She left her hood up, which kept her face and shoulders warmer, but also blocked her view of the road through town. Shop signs creaked ominously in the wind. At times, the noise muffled the sounds of carriages and wagons in the street.

"Miss Clay."

She turned, knowing whom she would see. The duke sat in a very smart curricle stopped at the nearest side of the street to her. His crest decorated doors of gleaming green lacquer. He'd put up the top to protect against the weather and turned up the collar of his greatcoat. He seated his whip and touched the brim of his hat. He managed to look dashing and forbidding at the same time.

She curtsied. "Your Grace."

"You are walking to Hope Springs?"

"Yes, Your Grace."

"In this weather?"

She glanced around and gave him a smile. "I haven't any other weather to walk in."

"I shall drive you home."

There was no dissuading him; she knew that. He had made his pronouncement, and no one defied him. There was, as well, the simple fact that she would much appreciate a ride, for it had turned colder than she liked. "Thank you."

He set the brake and dismounted. He was wearing his maroon boots, and they did look well on him. "No parcels, Miss Clay?"

She put her hand on his in preparation for stepping up. "I was at Mrs. Thomas's. For a meeting to finalize plans for the Christmas assembly."

"The Thomases?" He did not hide his astonishment.

"Yes." She smiled at him. "Is it true you never attend the assembly?"

"In previous years, I have had prior engagements."

Two steps up to enter, a quick grip atop the back of the seat, and she was on the bench. She imagined herself driving a curricle like this and thought the image rather fine. He swung up beside her. She gave him as much room as she could, but he was a man solidly built and wearing a thick coat. They would have a cozy drive to Hope Springs. "All the ladies think it a great pity that our leading citizen will not be in attendance. You will not reconsider?"

"It is not a matter to be reconsidered. A previous engagement is just that." The duke reached underneath the seat and took out a blanket. He shook it out and laid it over her legs, leaving it to her to cover her lap more fully.

"Thank you. You would attend, then, if you found you had no such engagements?"

"I cannot say. Perhaps." He settled onto the seat and took up his whip. In such close quarters, there was no help for the fact that his shoulder and thigh pressed against hers. "Why did you walk there?"

She considered an untruth but could not bring herself to lie to him. "I do not yet own a carriage."

He flicked the whip, and the horses started. Two bay geldings, matched in all particulars, including, she realized now, gait. His other hand tightened on the reins. "Why not?"

"It is an expense I had rather avoid just now."

"A necessary one for a woman who is sole head of her household."

She bowed her head and looked at him sideways. She did not expect him to be looking at her, but he was. "You are correct," she said. In all likelihood, this man would soon be her relative. "No one could be more correct."

"Which begs the question, why do you not have a carriage?"

"The expense. Taxes. I'd need another groom. I should want something smart, too. I know I would, and so I would spend too much. Then there are horses. They, too, are an expense."

He sent her a skeptical look, and she deserved every bit of that scorn. She did. "Have you spent all your money, then?"

"Of course not."

"I repeat my query."

"I confess it, Your Grace. I am over my head in this matter. Drowning." He would soon be in the place of head of her family. Its ranking member, once Louisa was his duchess. "Mr. Clay never let me drive, and I wouldn't know how to choose the right horses, the best for my money, and I don't wish to be taken advantage of. Suppose I buy a young horse when in truth it is not? I might buy a horse with a bad gait or a roarer or one not suited to a carriage, or that's bad-tempered or doesn't like women."

"Miss Clay—"

"One hears such terrible stories about old horses sold as young ones, or that have infirmities or other disorders foisted off on unsuspecting buyers. My own father famously paid over four hundred pounds for a stallion he meant to put to stud. The horse died of old age a week after the purchase."

"If you feel you would fall prey to such schemes, seek expert assistance."

"Whom am I to ask? I have been in Hopewell-on-Lyft a month. I do not know anyone well enough to ask for such help." She leaned her head back. "It isn't only horses, but everything. Everything. With every potential expense set before me, I fear I'll make the wrong choice."

"I doubt that."

"No?" She sat straight. "I do. I doubt passionately my ability to choose correctly."

He shook his head. Was that pity? Disgust? She could not tell.

"I ask you, what's to prevent me from losing my head and spending every penny I have on foolishness and fripperies?"

That earned her another scornful look.

"Cousin Clay was forever reminding me that my father had a fortune once and lost it with one terrible decision after another. He overspent, his investments went bad, he did not save, and then he married my mother, and that was unwise as well. I cannot tell you how unwise that was, according to him. Now I cannot shake the conviction that I, too, will find myself destitute and dependent. Again."

"Have you invested any of your money?"

"No." She wished she could melt into the fabric of the chair.

That answer earned her another astonished glance. "None at all?"

"Some in the five percents."

"There's that, then."

"Not enough. Not enough. What if I invest badly? Or not wisely enough?"

"I see no evidence you spend beyond your means."

"You don't know that." Where their bodies touched at shoulder and thigh, she was warm. Her feet were no longer as cold as they had been, and the blanket over her lap kept her legs warmer, too.

"No," he said after a short time had passed, "I do not."

"I bought insurance. Fire insurance."

"On Hope Springs?"

"Yes." Her stomach clenched. She did not wish to have a conversation that exposed her as baldly as this. All her faults for him to see.

"Fire insurance is not a reckless purchase."

"It might have been."

"Allow me to observe that your difficulty is not the decisions you make, but the ones you do not. You have not made purchases you ought to."

"I'm hopeless. Hopeless, I tell you."

He continued, unperturbed. "Delaying necessary purchases when you have the funds to make them is a false economy. If you fail to repair a leak, you will have a greater expense in future."

"I've already repaired the roof. And a chimney. And rebuilt the dairy."

"Do not despair. You are able to take decisions."

"I had not expected all those expenses at once."

He did not speak again until they were past The Duke's Arms, and Edith, having concluded the subject was dropped, turned her thoughts to happier ones of fashioning bouquets of mistletoe.

At the base of the hill, he gave his whip the lightest touch, and the horses moved in identical strides. A curricle like this, with horses as perfectly matched as these, would be a dream to own. How could she not look smart in such a curricle?

"I shall assist you."

"Gathering mistletoe, do you mean?" But, no. He could not mean that. She'd not told him of her need to gather mistletoe.

He gave her a puzzled look.

"Pay no attention. I've let my thoughts run away with me. I offered to gather mistletoe from Hope Springs as decorations for the assembly. But you could not have meant that, for I hadn't told you of my plans. What do you mean, you will assist me?"

"I shall assist you in the purchase of a suitable vehicle, the appropriate cattle, and in the hiring of an additional groom."

Yet more evidence of his intent to marry Louisa. If she were to find herself his relation, why, of course he would assist her. A man like him would consider it his duty. "I don't want to put you to any trouble."

"I shall present you with several choices and give you my reasoning for them. Once you've decided, I shall procure you the horses."

"That's generous of you."

His sideways glance told her he knew the reason for her hesitation. "Tell me what expense you cannot bear to exceed."

"Twenty pounds."

He laughed. "Will you drive a cart? Or a wagon? Pulled by an ass?"

"No." Her stomach clenched again, but then, if she could trust anyone's good sense and advice, it was the duke's.

"Well, then."

"I considered a curricle, you know. I think I should like one exceedingly." She ran a hand along the top of the door on her side. "Yours is so dashing."

"A curricle, Miss Clay, and suitable cattle will set you back more than twenty pounds."

"I do not need a coat of arms on mine. Nor gilt paint."

He turned down the drive to Hope Springs. "If you spend less than two hundred pounds, you will have nothing but regrets."

"Two hundred pounds?"

"For an amount nearer to what you wish to spend, I recommend a gig and a single horse."

"That will do, then."

He stopped his curricle before the house. "Very well, then."

Chapter Five

OXTHORPE FINISHED WITH Goodman two hours earlier than usual. They'd got through all his legal correspondence. Replies to letters requiring a response had been drafted and were ready to prepare for his signature. He'd reviewed ledgers and several investment proposals, all of which he had rejected. Goodman cleared his throat.

"Yes?" Why the devil did the man look as if he stood poised to drink hemlock?

"About your attendance at the upcoming festivities?"

"What festivities?"

His brow furrowed. "At St. Melangell's, sir."

Oxthorpe examined the point of his pen and, not to his credit, dissembled. "One's attendance at church is hardly festive."

"The Christmas assembly, Your Grace. At the parish hall."

"What about the assembly?" He no longer attended the assemblies. Not any of them. He donated generously. That was enough.

Goodman tugged on the bottom of his waistcoat and cleared his throat again. "But, Your Grace."

"Yes?"

"I have heard from several sources that your attendance is considered a positive fact."

"Your sources are incorrect." He dipped his pen in the inkwell as if he intended to write out one last letter. Goodman did not move. "I am otherwise engaged on the evening in question."

"Your Grace..."

He did not so much as glance at the man. "Good day to you, Goodman."

His solicitor bowed and took his leave. The door closed softly after him, and Oxthorpe found himself alone. Just as he preferred.

He put down his pen then picked it up again. Deuce take the Christmas assembly. He'd gone once and had been expected to enjoy himself. He had not.

He stared at the sheet of paper before him, his pen poised as if he were about to put ink to paper. He did have correspondence that ought to be written in his own hand. Letters he owed to friends and his few surviving relations, all elderly women. The invitation from Mr. Clay required his personal response. Or he could make his too-long delayed call at Hope Springs.

He had, in one of the drawers of his desk, the details of two suitable choices of conveyance for Miss Clay. These must be acted upon quickly if she was to secure her choice. Therefore, he was doing his duty by calling on her ahead of other tasks that were before him.

He cleaned and put away his pen and capped the ink then assembled the documents he'd compiled and gathered for her. He gave Mycroft instructions to have his horse brought around and went upstairs to change. If, while he was changing, he was more particular than usual about which breeches and coat, which gloves and whether his hair had been sufficiently tamed, his valet had no complaint of him for it. He wore his new boots.

With the documents tucked away in his coat, he went to the stable block. One of his grooms waited with his mare at the ready. Five minutes later, he was riding toward the border with Hope Springs.

There was no reason to believe he'd find Edith at any of the oaks on her property. It would be foolish to check since such a detour would take him a quarter of an hour out of his way. His mare, however, divined that his intentions and his desires were not the same, for she took the path toward the oaks, and he did not dissuade her.

He did not believe in fate, but good fortune? Yes.

She *had* told him she would be gathering mistletoe, after all. It would be his misfortune should he arrive at Hope Springs and find her out. If she was not at home, he must either wait or return to Killhope and delay his business with her, to her detriment. In light of that possibility, a thirty-minute delay in reaching Hope Springs was an excellent hedge.

He came over the rise and saw first the dark green shadows of the wood—then, among that dusky green, a flash of gold. His breath caught. If this was Edith, he hoped to God she was not in those dense oaks with no one to see to her safety. Not with the so called New Sheriff of Nottingham harassing and robbing both travelers on their way north or south as well as the good citizens of Hopewell-on-Lyft. A man desperate enough to train a gun on innocents would think nothing of trespassing on privately held, enclosed lands.

As he drew nearer, he made out a ladder leaning against the thick branch of an oak. The top of the ladder disappeared into the tree. To the right of the ladder was Edith's maid, looking up at the trees and whoever was on the ladder. Whether he'd seen the maid's gown when he saw that flash of gold, he could not say.

His fear that Edith herself was on the ladder was assuaged when she emerged from the trees. She held her bonnet in one hand and stood, eyes shaded with a hand, when he came close enough to speak. A breeze caught at her mantle and revealed a stripe of a yellow-gold gown.

He dismounted. From the look of things, she had been in the trees herself. Oak leaves and bits of moss clung to her hair and shoulders. He found the enthusiasm behind her untidiness quite charming. "Miss Clay."

"Good afternoon, Your Grace." Her eyes lit up, though there was no reason to believe she was pleased to see him, as opposed to pleased to see anyone at all. She curtsied. Her maid did the same and retreated several steps back. "What brings you here?"

Her ease around him was a consequence of her having no personal expectations of him; this he had understood from the start. She did not see herself as the sort of woman in whom he would take a personal interest. Nevertheless, he did not think it was his imagination that she was less formal with him than previously.

"I have information to put before you."

Leaves and smaller branches rustled, and Edith glanced into the tree. "Have a care."

"Below left!" came a masculine voice from the tree.

Her maid dashed to the other side of the ladder, a basket in hand. Something green dropped from the tree. The servant placed the basket to catch the mistletoe.

"Well done, Jim Dandy." Edith looked into the tree again. "Well done."

The man called down, "One more, and we've all we can take here, mistress."

"Good, good."

Oxthorpe walked toward the ladder and Edith. Beneath the branches, the ground was covered with oak leaves. There was no frost here. The maid stood on the other side of the ladder. Her basket was full of mistletoe, with the occasional twig or oak leaf among the leaves and berries. Nearby were three large bundles of mistletoe, tied up in squares of white cloth. "A good afternoon's work."

"Yes." Edith was cheerfulness itself. "Our assembly will have mistletoe everywhere you look."

That damned assembly. It wasn't enough that he donated the bulk of the funds or that he gave up his kitchen staff and cook for the duration. Not that he begrudged the expense or the inconvenience of a cold dinner, but every year he was bombarded with all manner of sly and not-so-sly hints that he attend. He had no wish to attend. He had, in fact, arranged to be away from Killhope at the time. "Ah, yes. You are on the committee."

"I am."

She would be there. At the assembly.

And he would not be.

"I have promised them mistletoe, and I mean for us to have more than you can imagine."

He glanced at the basket and the other bundles. "Success is within your grasp."

She laughed, and he was pleased to have amused her. "We've done a fine job here."

He brushed an oak leaf from her shoulder. "You have."

"We'll be the next week tying ribbons and lace."

"Why?"

"On the mistletoe. This year's decorative theme is blue and white grosgrain ribbon with blond lace."

"How festive."

"Yes, won't it be? I am so sorry you won't be there." She put her hands on her hips. "Never fear. I shall raise a glass of Mr. Wattles's famous cider and toast to your good health."

"Thank you."

She beamed at him. "Then I shall wish all present and future residents of Hopewell-on-Lyft and Killhope Castle a very merry Christmas and happy New Year. What do you say to that, sir?"

"Will you stand under the mistletoe and wait for a gentleman to kiss you?"

Her cheeks pinked up, and, good God. No. No. God, no. She thought he meant she would be waiting all night for such a thing. "That is not—"

"If Louisa were to come, there would be a line of gentlemen." She spoke too quickly, and her smile was gone.

"I daresay. Miss Clay—"

She took one of the leaves from the basket and held it up for inspection. "Did you ever see more perfect berries?"

Jim Dandy began his descent of the ladder. Instinctively, Oxthorpe steadied it. "Never," he replied to Edith, desperate to repair the damage he'd done. "Except at Killhope."

As the servant came down the last rungs, she laughed. "I say we repair to Killhope this instant and compare, for I'll warrant *my* mistletoe is the most perfect this side of the Vale of West."

He managed a smile. A small one. He took the mistletoe from her and examined it in the sun. He ought to go to the bloody assembly and kiss her beneath the mistletoe. *That* would cause a stir. "You will lose that wager, Miss Clay."

She stepped forward and squinted. "I would not. That mistletoe is perfect."

There was a moment when she stood underneath the mistletoe he held. The world swooped around him like a drunken lark. He ought to kiss her. One kissed a lady who stood beneath the mistletoe, though she hadn't done so on purpose.

Impossible. He could not do something so outrageous. In front of her servants. She would be offended. Or worse, she would endure the contact and ever after hold him in even greater dislike.

She might kiss him back. God, what if she did?

He lowered the mistletoe and tossed it in the basket. Behind this tableau of his hopes and her utter blindness to them, Jim Dandy put away the sickle he'd used to cut the plants from the tree and walked off with the ladder and two of the bundles of mistletoe, and that ended everything.

Her outing was done. Her maid covered the basket with a white cloth she tied to the handles to keep the mistletoe secure, picked up one of the other bundles, and followed in the steps of Jim Dandy. Offended, no doubt, on behalf of her mistress. Oxthorpe led his horse and walked beside Edith for the ten-minute return to Hope Springs. When they came near the stables, he handed off his horse to Jim, along with a coin for the servant's troubles on his behalf. "I shan't be longer than an hour. Give her water and hay, thank you."

"Your Grace."

He accompanied Edith into the house. She left him in the parlor, and he found he could not sit still. He paced the room, stared out the windows. Examined the walls and the repairs made to the chimney. He'd not seen the interior of the house since he and Goodman had made an inspection prior to its sale. She'd repainted and put up new curtains. The house had not come furnished, so that had been an expense that must have set off her spendthrift worries.

The furnishings she'd chosen reminded him of the woman who lived here. Nothing to admire, and yet he wished to be here. To stay here and be surrounded by rooms that settled him. He was at ease, and the longer he stayed, the more he found to like.

While he waited, taking in what she had done to make this her home, another maid brought in tea and a tray of biscuits, cold meats, and bread. He recognized her from Hopewell-on-Lyft. Edith came in shortly afterward. On his feet, he swept a hand toward the desk at one side of the room.

"I have drawings to show you." Without saying more, he walked to the desk and set his papers on the surface. "And a proposal for you."

Chapter Six

GOOD HEAVENS. EDITH gazed with some amazement at the scene in her parlor. The duke himself. In her house. She must remember every detail so that she could relay them to Louisa in her next letter. The Duke of Oxthorpe was seated at her desk as if he discussed business with her every day. Because he loved Louisa and wanted to be kind to his future relations.

Predictably, he took up all her attention. She wished Mrs. Quinn had not swooned over the man and thus made her so aware of his looks. Before, she had acknowledged that he was handsome. But now? Several times when he'd found her in the oaks, with leaves in her hair—could she have appeared any more undignified?—she'd lost her train of thought because she was struck by how green his eyes were. Or wondering if his hair was as soft as it looked.

Or whether he was a competent lover. Her mind went blank while her body flushed hot.

He looked over his shoulder at her, and his look of dry curiosity jolted her.

Confounded by that inappropriate reaction, she lifted the teapot and prayed God she did not look as stupefied as she felt. "Something to drink, Your Grace?"

He went back to his documents. "Thank you."

She poured his tea, which she knew he took plain. This fact she had observed during one of those interminable hours when he'd called on Louisa, and it had been her role to keep the conversation from dying.

Their fingers touched when she brought him a cup and saucer, entirely accidental, but her stomach lurched with recognition of him as a man. Behind the clothes, behind the title, he was a man who must have had lovers, who likely kept a mistress. Raven's wing-black his hair was, thick and glossy, and with a tendency to stand up after he'd run his hands through it. Which he had done twice.

He set his tea atop the desk and stood to hold a chair for her. She sat, and he fetched another chair for himself. She was no innocent. Once, just once, when she believed she would be forever bound to a dry and empty existence with her cousin she had taken a lover. They had neither of them thought their attachment would last beyond a few days. Then a few weeks. Two months. She had discovered the beauty of a man's body, the fit, the differences, astonishing uses for one's mouth. All that she'd put away when, at last, they'd parted ways.

Oxthorpe brought that roaring back, and it did not make sense. He loved Louisa. If he was here now, it was because of Louisa.

His attention flicked to her bosom. But no, that must be her imagination. She smoothed the lay of her skirts. Her gown was pink satin and gray silk with slippers to match and all in colors she loved because they suited her, because she had not been allowed to wear them before. As yet, she had little jewelry, but one of her first, early purchases had been a string of pearls that went well with this gown and her skin.

"Here are two choices for you." He laid out the papers he'd brought. The top two sheets were advertisements from a carriage maker in Nottingham. "Both these"—he pointed at the first—"are within your budget." He went through the respective costs, the taxes, the maintenance of each, the cost of the horse that best suited the purpose.

The information he'd run through threatened to slip away, and that was disconcerting. It was not her usual experience to find herself so flustered. He was not here for any reason but to do her a good turn. A man like him had no personal interest in a woman like her. She tapped the papers he'd put before her. "May I?"

"Yours to do with as you wish."

"Thank you." She studied the drawings and imagined herself in either of the gigs depicted on the sheets he'd provided. Both were small vehicles, but there would be room for her maid. He was right. Either would be an excellent choice. She went through the expenses he'd listed, written in a precise hand on a sheet of smooth, creamy paper.

Her stomach clenched again. The repairs to the house had just been settled, and here she was about to take on the expense of a gig, a horse, and another servant. She knew she ought to. She knew it. But she resented the need. She could buy something less expensive. She did not need to look smart or have a dainty mare. She could use one of the drays.

He put a hand on the papers. "Miss Clay, may I speak bluntly?"

"Please."

He shifted on his chair, and she was again pulled, unwilling yet enthralled, into recognition of him as a man. "You have been put to some expense, outfitting your house."

"I have." This was true, and his understanding of that settled her.

"You wish to economize." This, she realized, was his element, the managing of details. Choosing among facts and taking a decision.

"I do." She leaned an elbow on the desk. Her difficulties by the oaks were vanquished, the awkwardness she'd felt earlier now gone in the face of his competence here. "But I do not wish to be poor again."

"Economy is not always a savings."

She nodded. Again true. Nothing she did not know, yet, to her shame, knowledge she had been unable to put to use.

"A paradox it would seem, but true," he said. She was so accustomed to his brusque manner of speaking that she was taken aback by the lack of disdain in his reply. Taken aback and then grateful.

"Yes." She swallowed. "You are correct."

"If you do not buy the vehicle you need, then you will find yourself out the expense of what you buy now, in addition to what you must purchase later when you understand you do not have what you need. What is proper for a lady of means."

She met his eyes and did not see the usual chill there. "I could sell what I buy now."

"Not for the price you pay today."

She folded her arms on the desk and buried her head there. She squeezed her eyes closed then opened them and turned her head to the side of the desk where the duke sat. At least he wasn't mocking her. "Yes. Yes, yes, yes. You are right. I know you are right."

"Of course I am."

She sat straight, and then he smiled, and she drowned in her visceral reaction to that.

"Either of these would be suitable." He set a finger to the drawings. "If you permit me, I shall arrange the purchase and find you a horse."

One could admire a man's looks without thinking oneself his equal. She could. She had done so for all her adult life. "You are too generous."

"Not in the least." He drew a breath. "I have another suggestion."

"I am all ears."

"I have a curricle."

"The one I rode in, do you mean?" Yes. There. She had set aside the fact that his body was shaped by muscle. There was no denying him that, but she need not do anything but say to herself, *This is a fact about the Duke of Oxthorpe*, in the same way she would note that his coat was blue and his boots were maroon. "Is it awful of me if I tell you how much I enjoyed that?"

"No." His mouth twitched. "I mean another, however, which I have intended to take to a property I own in Northumberland."

Louisa. He meant his impending visit to offer for Louisa. What else could he mean? "The reason you will not be at the Christmas assembly."

"One of them, yes. I shall sell it to you, if you are interested."

"What is the other reason?"

"Affairs of business."

He'd answered her too quickly, and that got her thoughts stuck on his admission of more than one reason for going to Northumberland for the Christmas holidays. He quirked his eyebrows. She tipped her head to one side. The curricle was the excuse for his trip to Northumberland. If he did not wish to tell her yet about Louisa, she understood that. He was a private man. She understood that, too.

"How much?"

"Not what does it look like?" he asked, smiling again. "Not what is its condition?"

"I presume you are not scheming to sell me a wreck."

"No." He smiled again, distractedly, and tapped the larger of the gigs in the advertisements. "I propose to sell it to you for near what you would pay for this. I would, naturally, have it refinished to remove my coat of arms at no expense to you."

She gazed at the paper and felt her chest tighten. Every expenditure was a debit to her income, and they added up at an alarming rate. "Higher taxes. A greater cost."

"That is so." He sounded resigned.

"Two horses to keep rather than one."

"The curricle was custom made. To exacting specifications."

She raised her head from the papers he'd set before her. She wanted to. She did. But there was no need for a curricle, however dashing it would be. "Thank you for your generous offer."

His reply was a brusque nod.

"I sincerely mean that. I am flattered by your condescension and kindness. I need a carriage of some sort. But not a curricle when a gig will be more than sufficient for my needs."

"Miss Clay." He slouched on his chair, stretching out one leg. She swooned a little every time he smiled at her this afternoon, and now? With that slouch that spoke of a man at peace with his magnificent body? She was nearly insensate. "May I speak frankly yet again?"

"You may, but I must tell you it is not necessary to ask permission again. I hope and expect you will always speak frankly to me."

He tapped a finger on his thigh. She refused to look. She could not allow him to see her look. "You did not, until recently, have a fortune of your own. Nor any expectation of one."

"True."

"You do now."

"I do." Three times dead.

"You bought Hope Springs."

"I did, Your Grace."

He waved a hand to indicate their general surroundings. "This property suited your budget and your new future. Its purchase was an excellent decision."

"That was my opinion as well." She laughed and leaned toward him. Praise from the Duke of Oxthorpe. This was a day that must live forever in her memory. "I hope to live into my dotage, you see."

"So hope we all." He propped his elbow on the desk. "I presume your cousin was worse than useless after you came into your money."

She did not answer immediately, for the politics of her possible answer robbed her, momentarily, of her honesty. Then again, if he meant to marry Louisa, he must already know what her Mr. Clay was like. He was not the sort of man who would be fooled. "The change in my fortunes was, for him, a setback."

"No doubt." He met her gaze, smiling a little, and that sent her thoughts racing to what a man might do with his mouth. "You've no husband to manage your remaining funds."

That shocked her, that he would broach such a subject with her. "I have not."

"You would do better to marry than live here alone."

"I shall soon be twenty-eight. Not decrepit, but I haven't the youth gentlemen look for in a bride."

"A false statement."

"Well. Yes. Again, you are correct. After my good fortune became known, I refused the offers of six or seven gentlemen at least."

"Not one of them tempted you?"

"One or two, perhaps." She fell serious. "To marry in haste did not seem wise. My life was in such upheaval, and in all honesty, those who approached me or my cousin with offers were not gentlemen I knew well."

"That is a commendable caution." He lifted his gaze to hers. "No one you know well came forward?"

Her heart skipped. He could not know about her past or that she'd hoped, for a time, that the man who'd taken her to bed would call on her and lay his heart at her feet. He hadn't, and she'd been a fool to think he might. She had never been a suitable wife. They had not suited in that manner, and they'd both known it.

"If I were to marry—and I think that unlikely, sir—I had rather marry a gentleman whom I admire and respect."

"Someone who admires and respects you, one hopes."

"Yes. Precisely." She glanced down then back at him. He remained slouched on his chair, but everything else about him was alert.

"I shall write to my banker and my solicitor. Mr. Madison will reply because I shall have instructed him to do so. Consult with him and decide if you wish to put yourself in his hands. Mr. Goodman, my solicitor, shall call on you. He is at Killhope nearly every day."

Outside, the light changed as clouds moved across the winter sun. The shadows of his face changed with the light, and she thought of him lying in bed as the morning sun changed the light. "That is beyond generous. Thank you."

His response was immediate, and not what she expected from him. "I do not like your cousin, nor the way he behaved toward you."

Slowly, she frowned, and he met her gaze head on. "That is not Louisa's fault, you must know that."

He sat straight. "If you mean, did my dislike of him prevent me from making an offer I would have regretted, the answer is no."

Thank God. Thank God. Louisa's heart was safe. "You won't regret your decision. You won't."

"I assure you, I do not."

"I promise you, you will carry away the woman you love. What is a father-in-law you do not care for when you have all that your heart and soul require?"

His body stilled, and she had the awful premonition that she had said something he found objectionable. "Thank you for your advice."

She put a hand on his arm, desperate to repair the damage of her misstep, whatever it had been. "I'll write to Mr. Clay. I have nothing to lose by telling him he has made himself disagreeable to you. He will take measures. He shall. Do not allow one man's unpleasantness destroy your future happiness."

"I have no plans to do so." He retreated behind the cool green of his eyes, and her heart constricted. She'd said something wrong to make him so distant, and she'd give anything to know what. A clock somewhere near chimed the hour. "I'll take my leave. I shall arrange the purchase of the gig and a horse. Do not be astonished if I send a man round for you to interview. He will have a character from me."

"I'm sorry. I'm sorry if I've offended you."

"You haven't."

She searched his face, and he was impenetrable. Impassive. "Liar," she whispered, her chest tight.

They locked gazes, and she felt the connection to her toes. He reached for his tea, forgotten there on the top of the desk, and again she lost herself in the intensity of his eyes. "What a remarkable coincidence."

"Miss Clay?"

"The green of my china is an almost exact match for your eyes."

He held up his teacup and examined the color, and she did likewise, in that she studied the cup and then his eyes, and he obliged her by looking at her without blinking, and that made them both laugh. "Now you have taken your china into dislike."

"I haven't at all." Relief that he wasn't annoyed any longer made her giddy. "You have pretty eyes. I like my china even better now that I know the color is Killhope green."

"Am I to rest easy knowing that every night you'll take a knife in hand and think of my eyes?"

"Yes." She burst out laughing. "Yes, Your Grace. Every night an attack." Elbows on the desktop, she propped her chin atop her interlaced fingers. "I wish you would speak like this more often."

"I wish to stay on good terms with all my neighbors. And their knives." He put down his tea and straightened the papers he'd brought.

"I think I may be the only person alive who knows you are amusing."

"And I hope, Miss Clay, that you keep my secret."

Chapter Seven

OXTHORPE GAVE HIS horse its head, and his mare left the path and flew across the field. He'd had stallions with less strength and grace than his mare. She gathered herself to take the hedge, and they were airborne. Flying. They took the ditch between two fields, the stone fence after another. She knew the route for this morning's ride and kept her gallop another two hundred yards before she slowed and trotted to the path that would take them downhill to the Lyft.

The air was crisp, though last night's snow hadn't stayed on the ground. Another day of unusually mild weather for the time of year, then. Undoubtedly to be soon followed by a storm that would make them long for a day such as this one. As yet, the sky was gray with no threat of rain or snow.

Ahead of him, a hare darted from beneath the bramble on his left. His mount danced a bit, but she was not a horse that startled easily. The hare more slowly zigzagged across the grass in the direction of yet more bramble. Not a hare, after all. From the looks of the creature, an Angora rabbit: someone's escaped livestock. He did not keep Angoras, though for all he knew, Miss Clay did.

The pond that marked a portion of the boundary between his property and Miss Clay's came into sight. If he were to look behind him, he would see the distant towers of Killhope. Were he to continue downhill and past the pond, he'd end up at Hope Springs where only a faint curl of smoke revealed its location.

Legally, the pond was his, but previous occupants had for years been permitted to fish here. Edith, however, was unlikely to lay claim to that right. He would have to mention he did not mind if she sent her gamekeeper to fish there. She'd hired a local man into the position vacated by the previous gamekeeper, who'd retired when the property changed hands. A word with him might be in order on that subject, as well as an inquiry about wayward Angoras.

He dismounted on the Killhope side of the water, away from the stream that fed into the Lyft. When he returned to Killhope Castle, it would be to ten years of work to be done in a day. Letters to sort, documents to read. Accounts, reports, and bills to review. Letters to write: a mile of them. Even here in the country, so far from London, there would be callers to meet and appointments to keep.

If it were any season but winter, he'd go for a swim and delay his return to duty. He examined the water. Barely a ripple across the surface. Any ice there might have been earlier in the morning had long melted. The day was cold, but not freezing. There was no reason not to brave one last swim of the year.

He stripped off and laid his clothes on shrubs near where his horse examined the vegetation for edible shoots. Which his mare found. Naked, he waded into the water. Cold. Damned cold, but not freezing. He'd taken colder baths in his life. Either he was man enough to face the cold or not. He struck out and stroked as fast as he could, pushing himself.

Faster than his usual pace, for he wanted the heat of exertion, the burn of muscles used. Faster. Faster yet. He reached the other side, gasping, used up and glad for every thud of his pulse. He stood in hip-deep water, wishing he had someone here to time him. He had not swum so fast in all his life. The snap of cold air cut through him, invigorated him, reminded him he could feel. He stood, eyes closed, face turned to the sky. He did feel.

"Duke."

He knew her voice without looking. A calming timbre, and so often with a hint of amusement. In London, and later in Tunbridge Wells, he had often fancied no one but him heard that sliver of wit. How could any man hear that and not be fascinated? He did not move. One did not display one's nude body to a woman whom one was not about to take to bed. It was unlikely that would happen. But, well. The damage was done, wasn't it? Most of his privity was under water.

"You are on my side of the pond."

Hands on his hips, he looked at her. The world went from gray to colors—the backdrop of green fields and woods behind her. Ebony cloak with a flash of ermine lining, a dress of bronze and green, gloves to match the green.

He said, "Killhope lands include the pond."

He did not want to go to his grave knowing he had risked nothing for the woman he wanted. He wasn't an ass, though. Or if he was, he did not wish to give her incontrovertible evidence of the fact. What to say to her, then, when he knew he was likely to speak too gruffly?

She cocked her head, cheeks pink from the cold he did not yet feel. "Does that mean I have less property when the water is high and more when it's low? That hardly seems fair."

"I'll have the survey copied for you." A safe reply. As dull as that stack of correspondence in his office.

She pursed her lips and then smiled like it was spring. "It's not as if I shall raise an army and battle you for possession."

He returned her gaze. "If this were Edward's time," he said, "or Elizabeth's, or any of the Henrys, I'd marry you, and the property would be mine."

She broke into a grin. "You'd come to my house in the dead of night and carry me off?"

He willed her to understand how little this was in jest. "I would appeal to my sovereign and come away with a royal decree that we wed immediately."

"A better solution than armies poised to battle." She stood several feet from the edge of the pond. Gaze averted. He'd seen that absent look from her dozens of times in London. She thought herself invisible and was not. Not to him. This was the second time he'd mentioned marriage to her. The second time she heard nothing but his words.

"At any rate," she went on, "I shan't dispute that you are currently in the water, whichever of us it belongs to. But you'll catch your death if you stay there."

"I won't."

"It is winter, Your Grace. And as you once sagely advised me, only a fool goes out in the cold."

He had a mad urge to wade out of the pond and—what sort of monster imposed his naked self on a woman? She would not appreciate a display of male nudity she had not asked to encounter. She hadn't asked and wasn't about to, for pity's sake. He stayed in the water. "It is not cold."

Steadfastly, she smiled at the vista to her right. "How odd, do you not agree, that we two are within ten feet of each other and have entirely different experiences of the temperature?"

"No."

"It cannot be significantly colder where I stand."

The wind picked up, and the cold bit hard enough to prickle the surface of his skin. He willed himself not to rub his arms.

She peeked at him, and her eyes widened. "Shall I fetch your clothes?"

"No." He ought to say something more. Do something. But what? Swim away? That seemed abrupt.

No one had expected him, of all men, to pay attention to a woman who wasn't young anymore, who had no fortune, and who was not particularly handsome. He hadn't. Not at first. She had been nothing. A companion to her sig, the young lady whom others thought he ought to marry. He'd thought so himself, until he'd spent more time in conversation with her than Miss Louisa Clay.

What to say? He had no experience with situations like this. He had no difficulty with women. In the main, he didn't. He had a mistress he liked well enough, at present in London. She entertained him in bed because he made it convenient for her to be there exclusively. They understood their relationship and its boundaries.

He imagined himself saying, *May I ask a favor of you?*

And she, not knowing what he intended, would likely reply, *Shall I fetch your clothes?*

He could point to the other side of the pond and say, *Would you go there, take my watch, and time how long it takes me to swim back?*

She'd hurry to his clothes and find his watch. She'd raise her hand as a signal to prepare himself, and he would wave back and prepare himself for the return swim. He'd swim the way he had before, fast and faster yet, and when he reached the other side, he'd stand, water sluicing off him.

She'd clutch his watch, all smiles, and God save his soul, he wouldn't care in the least that her smile came at the cost of his dignity. His dignity could go to the devil if it meant she smiled because of him. *A record*, he'd say. *My fastest swim yet.*

None of that happened.

None.

Because it was unthinkable that he could ask her that. If he did, he'd not manage the right words nor speak in the right voice. He'd imply she would steal his watch while she did him this ridiculous, absurd, undignified favor that presumed a familiarity between them that did not exist.

She would feel, as he did, that such a question was inappropriate and unbecoming of him. Insulting. He shivered, once.

Before him, she sent a rueful look to the skies. "Forgive me for keeping you." She curtsied. "Good day to you, Your Grace."

"Miss Clay." He watched her stride away, and only when she was out of sight did he make the return swim to the Killhope side. He was bloody cold and never so glad in all his life that he not been a fool.

He could not have borne her thinking him a fool.

Chapter Eight

A GENTLEMAN'S BOOT stood directly in Edith's way. She was on the path that led from the rear of Hope Springs and wound upward to the ridge above the Vale of West. The boot was upright, as if the owner had carefully placed it there to fend for itself, the devil may care for its fate. Precisely and exactly there. It was maroon leather and an exact match for the one-half of a pair of boots that had been deposited in her driveway the day she'd walked to The Duke's Arms and met Oxthorpe himself. How odd to encounter it again. Here. A walk of many minutes from her house—or Killhope for that matter.

She was halfway through a favorite ramble of hers that took her past the pond, though not to it, and up the hill with a view of the vale that took her breath every time she saw it. A thin layer of snow covered the ground, already more melted than not. The grass remained crunchy with frost.

She had no expectation she would again encounter the duke here, naked or otherwise. This was now in doubt. Here was his boot. Might not more of his clothing be nearby?

She picked up the boot and detoured to a point where she could see enough of the pond to determine whether the duke was there and might merely have dropped his boot. However, she saw no sign of Oxthorpe or his clothing.

Killhope was half a mile distant. Hope Springs was a mile and a half away. She set off for the castle with his boot tucked under her arm. Though the castle sat atop a hill that made the towers visible from most everywhere in Hopewell-on-Lyft, much of the structure was hidden by dense growths of oaks and pines. At the border between the two properties, the footpath she'd been following turned to a groomed path that led downhill and then, abruptly, uphill to the castle.

She emerged from the tree-shaded path into a meadow that would have been pretty but for the forbidding stone walls of Killhope at the other side. A driveway of finely crushed and raked gravel swooped around from the front and led to the stable block to her right.

The rear gates—tall, black ironwork with a griffin on the left side and a swan on the right—were open. Massive wooden doors were locked in place against the stone walls. As she walked through the gate, she felt very small indeed and unduly aware of the holes above through which Oxthorpe soldiers would have poured boiling water or oil onto enemies.

Killhope's inner courtyard, bisected with a raked gravel path that led to the front doors, also open, could have held an army. Not so long ago, it surely must have. The Fletcher family had begun their history of nobility as original Earls of the Marches. Groomed lawns filled the spaces between the drive and cobbled walkways that led to various wings of the castle, or to the well, or to the cannons chained to the walls and still trained on the countryside below. Perhaps in expectation of another Cromwell?

To her right, across the courtyard, the front gates were taller yet, and not two wooden doors, but one of wood painted black. A massive iron chain held up the portcullis. The duke's banner flew from the wall above, flapping in the breeze. Everything she saw here was tidy and clean. Even the cannons were immaculate.

She did not, however, see a servant to whom she could entrust the duke's boot. Smoke curled from the chimneys, and curtains had been drawn, so it wasn't as if no one was home. She considered leaving the boot in the middle of the courtyard, perhaps atop the cover to the well. There would have been a lovely irony in that. She did not.

She walked toward the front gates and found the wooden steps to the entry door. At one time those steps would have been portable, to be put away in the case of a siege or attack. She stood on the top stair facing a brass door knocker in the shape of a swan. She was forced to admit that Killhope, so far, was not the dreary, ancient heap of stone she'd imagined.

The duke's butler, one Mycroft, opened the door at her knock. From time to time, she saw him in Hopewell-on-Lyft on the duke's business, and she'd seen him in The Duke's Arms lifting a pint with her butler when they happened to share the half day her cook was off, too.

Mycroft gave a smile that did not suit the reputation of his most cold and forbidding of employers. "Good morning, Miss Clay."

She extended the boot with one hand and pointed in the general direction of Hope Springs with the other. "I found this."

He took the boot from her and examined it for new dents in the leather. "Thank you, miss. It was kind of you to bring it here."

"Has anyone considered buying the dog its own boot?"

"Ah, miss, what haven't we tried? Several times already, we've relocated where the footmen polish His Grace's boots. It seems she's a particular fondness now for these boots." He leaned in. "No others will do now. I fear she believes the boots are hers."

"Dear me." Behind Mycroft was an enormous arrangement of roses—white and red and pink—each bloom or bud perfectly formed. Fern leaves had been added to the arrangement, too. You'd think it was the middle of spring here instead of winter. "Oh," she said. "Oh, those are the most beautiful roses I have ever seen in my life."

Mycroft stood aside, and she walked straight to the table and breathed in. "They smell wonderful." She breathed in again. "How thoughtful to put them here where guests may be delighted by them." Privately, she wondered how many guests a man like the duke might have to be delighted, with or without roses. Social callers, not business callers.

"His Grace insists, miss."

"Is that so?" The duke did not seem the sort of man to care about flowers. What an unexpected discovery, that he should insist on such a thing. From duty, no doubt, not for reasons of aesthetics, surely. Then again, he possessed a sense of humor that perhaps no one but she had witnessed. Was it not possible that there was more to him than she thought? "How is anyone growing roses in winter? My garden is completely fallow. Everything cut back to the root. I haven't a single leaf or flower."

"A conservatory."

She froze, for that was not Mycroft's voice. She turned her back to the flowers, and there he stood. Not naked. Heavens, she could not erase that image from her mind. He wore tan breeches, a gold waistcoat worked with tiny red dots, and a carelessly tied neckcloth. His buff coat made his eyes colder than morning frost. He wore a perfectly good pair of boots. Entirely serviceable. Because, as she knew, he did not have both his top boots.

"A conservatory." She had seen him nude. Nearly nude. Standing in the water. A naked duke. "Yes, what else could it be but that?" For the second time, she was flustered by her reaction to him. "I ought to have guessed."

That flicker of something in his eyes surely meant he agreed she should have. A handsome man, yes, but so cold, so haughty, she could never entirely dismiss the uneasiness she felt around him. In London, she'd been as uninteresting to him as she was to any other gentleman who called on Louisa. She'd been impressed by his rank, of course, but all she need do in those days was give him his due respect, and that was that. *Good day, Miss Clay*, he'd say in his somber way, and she would smile and say, *Good day, sir*, and he'd turn to Louisa, who was too often struck dumb, and bow to her. *How lovely you and your cousin are today.*

Of all the gentlemen who called on Louisa, the duke had been both the most terrifying and fascinating. When it became clear his interest in Louisa was more than incidental and that there would surely be a match between them, it had been Edith's duty to chaperone. With Louisa unable at first to be herself when the duke was present, Edith had found much of the conversational efforts had fallen to her. She had been happy to do so, happy to watch her cousin slowly relax into her natural, gracious habits around the duke.

"I wish you good morning." She bent a knee. "I have returned your missing boot."

His gaze flicked to his butler, holding the boot. He was an overweening presence here, too, just as he had been in London and Tunbridge Wells. And her drawing room. No one else mattered now that he stood here with his chill eyes. A little of Louisa's trepidation crept up on her.

"I must be on my way. Good day to you, sir." She nodded at Mycroft. "Good day."

The duke tipped his head backward. "You will see the conservatory."

The authority of the words caught at her, wrapped her up in his imperative. She did not wish to. Not in the least. She opened her mouth to make an excuse, but Mycroft cleared his throat. "You will much enjoy such a tour, Miss Clay."

She dismissed as absurd the notion that the butler meant to smooth over his employer's gruffness, and that it was done from fondness for the man. She could not imagine an unhappier place to work than Killhope Castle. Nor a more cheerless employer—except he was not dour all the time. He wasn't.

"May I take your cloak, Miss Clay?" Mycroft gave her such a desperate, plaintive look that she could not bring herself to beg off.

She handed over her cloak. For Louisa's sake, anything. "I should be delighted."

Mycroft folded her cloak over his arm and accepted her hat as well. She shook out her walking dress and reached up to secure a few hairpins that had come loose during her walk.

"This way." The duke strode off, and she hurried after him. She caught up but had to lengthen her stride to keep pace with him.

The interior of the castle was nothing like her imagination. The dank walls and darkened rooms of her imagination did not exist here. The tapestries hung on the walls had not been drizzled and thus retained the glitter of gold and silver thread and did their part in keeping the cold at bay. Sconces and candelabras contained beeswax tapers, and there was mirrored glass to reflect light. As they walked, they passed a niche with a suit of armor, and it occurred to her that one of his ancestors must have worn that gleaming steel.

She knew his history, or at least the history most often repeated about him. His father had died before Oxthorpe's birth. His mother had left him in the care of tutors and advisers and passed away the day after he reached his majority. Though he had not been an orphan, the fact was he had lived his life here, without either parent. "You grew up here, sir?"

He gave her a cold look. "Yes."

"At Killhope, I mean to say."

"I did."

She imagined a young boy with dark hair and pale green eyes wandering the corridors and passageways, alone, with no one but tutors and servants to keep him company and entertain him. No wonder he was so solitary a man, if he'd grown up here with no friends or boys his age.

He stopped at a set of double doors carved with a swan on one side and a griffin on the other. He opened the door with the griffin and held it for her. "You ought to have sent a servant."

She kept her smile. She must. One did not insult a duke. She had no wish to insult anyone, least of all a neighbor, and even less one who owned most of the land for miles. "In future, I shall know better."

He set off down a short, wide corridor hung with paintings she would have loved to study. "I hope so."

That was too much. Edith glared at his retreating back. "I have done you a service as well, Your Grace."

He stopped walking and faced her. "What service is that?"

"I have twice found and returned your footwear."

"I have acknowledged that."

"I ought to have left your boot where I found it."

"As I said." He spoke with infuriating calmness.

"And you say I ought to be married." She shook her head. "You, sir, are sadly and badly in need of a woman's gentle influence."

"I do not deny that."

She gave him a sideways look. "You understand your shortcomings in this respect and take no measures to remedy them?"

"There we must disagree."

She could not help smiling. "Then you *do* intend to go to Holmrook for Christmas."

"I have made no such decision. Is that the reason for your sharp tone, Miss Clay?"

"No, sir, it is not." There was no more maddening man on this earth.

"May I inquire what I have done to offend you?"

"You are a duke, yes. I acknowledge that I am nothing and no one compared to you."

His dark eyebrows drew together. "I hope I have not given you cause to believe such a thing."

"It's true. There's no point pretending it isn't. You were kind to offer your assistance in the matter of my crisis of transportation."

"Thank you." But his words dripped ice.

"Neither of those things mean I welcome you sharing your low opinion of my decisions."

"I feel," he said, "that you do not refer to my criticism of your lack of decision about a carriage."

"Don't be willful."

"Never."

Hands on her hips, she said, "I felt it was more expedient and convenient to you, sir, to return your boot myself rather than walk all the way home and ask one of my servants to bring it here."

"My apologies, Miss Clay, for giving offense. I did not intend that."

Her stomach dropped to her toes. His eyes, such a cold and pale green, were really quite remarkable. When he looked at her, it was like being taken apart from the inside out.

"But it is very much the case that you could have left it there."

"No, sir," she said softly. She could not—would not—tolerate his treating her in this dismissive fashion, as if she were as cold as the blood that ran in his veins. As if she cared for nothing but rational decision. "I could not have."

He let out a long breath. "I suppose not."

What was she to make of that flicker of resignation in his reaction? "I would not have left anyone's boot in the field. Not even yours."

"One of the servants would have gone in search of it."

"I found it first."

"So you did." He turned away. At the end of the corridor, he opened one of a pair of doors that were twins to the ones at the other end, with the same beautiful carving of his coat of arms. Again, he held the door for her.

Even before she passed him, she smelled roses, and then she forgot the petty irritations of her exchange with the duke.

"Oh. Oh." She stood inside, entranced.

The door he'd held for her opened onto a lengthwise oval of paradise, a more recent addition to the castle, for nothing like this would have been attached to a structure meant to instill dismay and despair in attacking armies.

A passion vine wound around a marble arch to her left. Opposite that was an orange tree. Roses grew along the entire long side of the oval. White gave way to pink gave way to red. A climbing rose with white blossoms streamed along a column and over a limestone arch.

To her right, a servant knelt in one of the beds, and not far from him a black-and-white collie lay on her side. He saw them, put away his shears and the rest of his implements, and edged toward the bare outline of a door meant to blend into the wall. The collie followed, hopping on three legs.

Edith walked farther in. Delighted. Astonished. "How do you get them to bloom this time of year?"

"Paling."

This proved to be the servant's name, for the man turned and bowed to the duke. Like Mycroft, he did not seem fearful or terrified of his employer. "Your Grace."

"See to it that Miss Clay has roses to take home with her."

"Sir."

"Hardly necessary." That earned her another icy look. "But—that would be lovely. Thank you."

Paling had already retrieved a bucket from some hidden cavity, and now he pulled his shears from a pocket and headed for the roses.

"Have you a favorite color, Miss Clay?"

"They're all so lovely, I could not possibly choose."

"That is not an answer."

No man could have more thorns than he. Either he was silent as a block of ice or on the verge, she was certain, of telling her how deeply he disliked her and wished she would stay away. "Pink."

"Plenty of the *Duchesse de Montebello*, Paling."

That he knew the names of the roses disconcerted her. The duke of her slowly crumbling imagination was not a man who knew such things. Not a man whose servants would smile. Yet. And yet. He had offered to help her buy a gig. And a horse. She had seen him naked, near naked, all pale skin and muscled body. Adonis rising from the water. He had made her laugh. More than once.

These were not feelings she ought to have where he was concerned. She did not wish to think of him as a man. She couldn't.

To put some distance between them, she walked toward the marble stairs that led to an interior terrace. Here, there were two upholstered benches, several chairs, and a table. To her left, a wide and tall glass door with a pointed top was closed against the winter air, but here he'd cleared the trees to unblock the view of the Vale of West. At the far left edge of the window glass, she could see one of the castle walls. That marble terrace meant that in summer and spring one might sit outside and admire the prospect.

Was it possible he sat here in awe of the view? Surely not. Surely. But how could he not, in the face of such beauty? The view swept her away, took her breath and her words. Heedless of her audience, uncaring, she stood in the center of this terraced view and spread her arms wide. Head back as she breathed in, she turned in a circle.

She ended up facing the duke. He remained on the landing above the stairs. She lowered her arms, and he flushed. If she hadn't known better, she would have thought him embarrassed. What could possibly make a duke uncertain of himself? She smiled at him and forgave him every cross look and word they'd ever exchanged. "Mycroft was right. I have enjoyed this. Thank you for showing me this. I am glad, so glad, you insisted."

He nodded. A curt movement of his head, and she was, for no reason at all, convinced that the man before her was not in dislike of her but simply a man who did not have words come easily to him because he'd grown up alone.

She thought of him as a boy. Lonely here, with no father and no mother to hold him, only the servants for company, and Killhope as an unceasing reminder of the centuries of duty and responsibility that were his. Her heart twisted up.

Chapter Nine

IF HE SPOKE, there was no possible outcome but another disastrous exchange of words at cross-purposes. The chances of his finding both the right words and the right inflection were, in his experience with her thus far, vanishingly small. He would either growl at her, or tell her what was in his heart. She wasn't some young girl who would accept a proposal of marriage from him merely because a duke bent a knee to her. God in Heaven, he would not want her to be such a woman.

He floundered in the waters of his admiration for Edith. Men like him married for the suitability of the match. They married young, to secure the line of inheritance. They married nobility, or else for reasons of money, property, and politics. He'd done none of that. None. The thought of doing so now turned him dead inside.

There was merit in a marriage made for reasons of duty. Until Edith, he'd intended to make just such a marriage. Had his life not taken such an odd turn, he might this moment be married to a woman—likely Miss Louisa Clay—who would have accepted him for reasons of his rank rather than her heart. He would have had no quarrel with that result. They would have made the pattern from which others might make similar marriages of suitability.

Then, Jesus, weeks after his hopes for Edith lay in tatters, after days and days of rumors and gossip about the men who had offered for her once her circumstances were so changed, she'd inquired about Hope Springs. This he'd learned solely because of his insistence on reviewing with Goodman the details of his estate.

For ill or good, he'd picked up the letter from her solicitor to his and said, "This offer."

Now he feared what the future might bring. That leaden weight in place of his heart was dread that she'd moved here because she believed he would marry her cousin and hoped to be close to Miss Clay without making a nuisance of herself. Dread that she would meet some other man and see in him all the joy of life that he lacked.

"I shall see you home." The words came out all wrong, with gruff emphasis on the word *will*. One look at her, and he lost all chance at serenity. Because he had never in his life cared whether anyone liked him. He'd never thought about it. Until her.

She intended to tell him no. Because that was her way. Because she was worried he might throw over her cousin on some whim or other. She was not wrong in that, since, in fact, he did mean to. Just the other day, when he'd felt the delay in a response to Clay's invitation was yet another message, he'd replied to the man's letter, which included a breezy, amusing paragraph from Louisa. In his single-paragraph reply, he wished Clay and his daughter all the happiness of the coming holidays and ended with the dry fact that he intended to remain at Killhope until February or March and then remove to Wales until June.

He presumed Clay would understand his letter for the rejection it was. He took a breath. "It is cold."

She touched a near blossom. "You admit that, do you?"

"There have been six robberies between here and Hope Springs."

"Not in daylight."

"Two."

She glanced at him. "Not recently."

"Tuesday last. And Friday."

"I never heard that."

"The road goes through the woods not once but twice." He held back a fierce smile when he saw the moment she acknowledged he was correct. "Nor will I send you home with flowers to manage on your own."

"In that case, thank you." She curtsied, and it was well done, in that way that never yet failed to make his heart clench.

It was her grace that had first caught his eye. That and the fact that three weeks into the Season, everyone he knew, lady or gentleman, had eventually remarked in passing that they very much liked Miss Edith Clay, and wasn't

Miss Louisa Clay a pretty young thing? Men wrote poems in praise of Miss Clay's beauty, but they all wanted Edith to sit beside them at dinner.

On their return journey through the house, he stopped a servant and asked to have his carriage brought around. In this he was fully competent. He could instruct his staff without losing himself. He gave instructions. They were carried out.

They resumed their walk with him infernally aware of her keeping pace. Her gaze moved from place to place, to open doors, to statues occupying niches, to the chandeliers and sconces. Doubtless, she had imagined he lived in a dungeon, a moldering heap where the blood of ancient enemies yet stained the floors. He'd heard the talk. The local stories, most too fanciful by far, about how his home had come to be called Killhope.

He stopped at the next door. "The saloon." He refused to look at her. "The second level I added three years ago." He pointed to the open second level with a walkway and walls lined with shelves of books. He could propose to her. She might accept because of his rank. Because he was Oxthorpe. She might. He thought, hoped, desired that if she did, she would eventually come to love him. If she didn't? If she never loved him? No fate could be worse than life without her regard. He'd rather live without hope of her love if her marriage to another man brought her happiness.

"Do you entertain here often?"

He wanted to put her back to the wall and take her mouth. He wanted to hold her tight and see where that led them. He knew how to kiss a woman. A lady. Even with the raw edge of lust there, he could kiss her. Wanted to, at any rate. "No."

They continued in silence. He stopped at the drawing room and stood by the door while she wandered a few feet inside. She turned in a slow circle, head up, for it was the frescoed ceiling that made this room a delight. "I am transported."

She spoke softly, in awe, and when she focused on him, he gave a brusque nod in return.

"If I had such a ceiling as this, I would lie on the floor hours of every day."

"I might have done so."

She tipped her head to one side, plainly working out if he'd spoken in jest or was serious.

"In my youth."

Somehow, he had not bungled his response, for she appeared genuinely delighted with their exchange. "A well-spent youth."

"Yes."

Their last stop was a smaller drawing room, his favorite room to sit with the morning *Times* and a sporting paper or two. He'd placed his favorite chair where there was a glimpse of the Lyft wending its eventual way to the pond between their respective properties. The rest was obscured by the woods where some damned fool was playing at highway robbery and calling himself the New Sheriff of Nottingham.

"How pleasant it must be to sit here with such a prospect to admire." She looked over her shoulder at him, as ever, not in the least affected by him or his consequence. Not one whit. She was a lady, yes, but she would never believe herself the sort of woman who might marry a duke. "You aren't the sentimental sort, are you?"

"I'm told not."

She considered him, and he felt the curiosity behind her scrutiny of him. He had no idea what to make of that and so pushed off the wall he'd leaned against and headed for the door. She followed.

By the time they reached the entry, Mycroft waited with her cloak and hat in hand. A footman held the roses, securely wrapped in paper and tied with string. A suitably large arrangement, he was pleased to see. The roses wouldn't last much longer this time of year. Paling had worked a bloody miracle getting so many blooms out of season.

Having assisted her in donning her cloak, Mycroft produced Oxthorpe's greatcoat. While he shrugged into it, he heard his carriage arrive in the courtyard. He accepted his hat and pulled his gloves from his pocket. Mycroft glided forward and opened the door.

The air was crisp and clear, though a breeze carried a few wisps of smoke into view. He assisted Edith into the carriage then entered himself and accepted the roses from the footman. He handed them to her.

She laid them on her lap and put a hand on the strap to brace herself when the coachman snapped the reins. The interior now smelled of roses. They were half the distance to the road before either of them spoke.

"We shall have more snow soon," she said.

"Yes."

"This is my first winter in Nottinghamshire." She smiled. "Is this weather unusual for the time of year?"

"No."

She bent her head over the flowers. He knew she was not beautiful. He knew she did not see herself as the object of a man's lust. He knew if he told her he found her desirable, she'd not understand his meaning. She'd think he meant something other than marriage. In that, she would be right, but a man could want both things from the same woman. "They're lovely."

Silence descended. Her cloak was good wool. Thick and inky black. It would do for a Nottinghamshire winter. Her boots were sensible, too. Solid construction for walking. He approved of how she'd spent her money to outfit her wardrobe.

"What did you feel when you understood you held the winning ticket?"

Slowly, she lifted her head, and their gazes connected. This time, he did not look away from her. He wanted this atom of truth from her. "I was shaking." She held out a hand. "Trembling. Cold and hot all at the same time. I must have read the numbers a hundred times. I was lightheaded."

"You did not swoon."

"No, though I wonder I didn't. I ought to have." She pressed the back of her hand to her forehead and fluttered her eyes. "If ever there was a time a woman should swoon, it's when she's won seventy-five thousand pounds in the lottery."

"Not you."

"No." That was agreement with him. She held up a hand, palm down. Her fingers shook. "Look." Her words were soft, so soft and, yes, that was a quiver. "I'm atremble at the recollection."

Reckless abandon washed over him, and he wrapped his fingers around hers. "As would anyone be."

"Not you."

He waited too long to reply, for she tugged on her fingers. But he did not release her hand. "Once," he said, aware he was taking the conversation into dangerous waters, "I won ninety-seven thousand at faro."

Her eyebrows drew together. "Faro?"

He released her hand. And there went any improvement in her opinion of him. Of all the fool things to confess, why that?

"Recently?" She let go the strap.

"I was seventeen, and it was the first time ever I set foot in a"—he almost said *bawdy house*—"gaming establishment."

"Oh." Her cheeks pinked up. She understood the sort of place he'd been.

"And the last."

"You were seventeen. Oh, reckless youth."

"I was perfectly sober."

"Ninety-seven thousand pounds."

He nodded. The blacklegs and Mollies had done their utmost to keep him in the house—spirits, food, women, men, and promises of perversions involving all of those things. The women had got him in the door, but they could not prevent his leaving. "I collected my winnings." Vowels, banknotes, and two deeds. "And I went home. Every day I send my thanks to the heavens that I made it home without being robbed."

Her eyes widened, and then the grin she'd been fighting broke out. "From a youth who gazed hours at such a marvelous ceiling to one who stood at a faro table."

"An indiscretion of youth never to be repeated."

"Ninety-seven thousand pounds." She whispered the numbers as she settled a hand around her throat. "Goodness. What if you'd lost?"

"You may believe that I did not speak of it to anyone."

She bit her lower lip and looked at him from beneath her lashes. His stomach swooped to his toes. "I did not tell a soul. No one, until my winnings had been deposited in the bank. And even then, I visited my banker to be sure I would be allowed to withdraw funds."

"As you were."

"I was, and it was the most"—she closed her eyes but opened them again immediately—"the most wonderful freedom. I stood in the Bank of England, five one-pound notes in my pocket. More money than I'd ever had in all my life, and it was mine."

Five pounds lost from his pocket would be nothing to him, though by nature he would both know and resent the misplaced funds. He could imagine, but never understand, a life where five pounds represented a vast fortune. The fact was, his last quarter's income had approached thirty thousand pounds sterling. One of those damned deeds he'd won as a feckless seventeen-year-old had been to a lead mine that added a tidy sum to his balance sheets.

Edith leaned toward him. There was a connection between them, true and real. "I shall confess something to you, but only if you promise never to breathe a word to another soul."

"Unless you confess a crime." The rich blue of her bodice looked well on her. Very well. She'd a wardrobe of color now, instead of those plain and sober hues.

"A failing of character that breaks no laws, though perhaps that's worse."

He nodded. The carriage began the descent that would take them through the first of the woods before the bridge into Hopewell-on-Lyft.

"My cousin Mr. Clay was cross with me when I came home that day. He felt I'd taken an unwarranted liberty being gone so long, and he took me to task. I'd taken one of the upstairs maids with me, you see, and she was wanted while we were out." She touched her upper chest. "But I listened to him tell me how ungrateful I was for all that he'd done for me those many years, and I thought to myself, I have five pounds in my pocket that did not come from him. I am wealthy now. Wealthier than he. I said too pertly, I confess it, 'Mr. Clay, Cousin, I am removing from your house this day.'"

"And?" What a moment that must have been for her. If he'd been there in witness, he'd have cheered her on.

"And—" She sat back, quite satisfied with herself. "Well, sir, I hired away the maid and one of the footmen, and we three removed to the Pulteney Hotel, where we stayed until I purchased Hope Springs. Mr. Clay called on me once to tell me again how ungrateful I was. In a pique, I sent him a hundred pounds in repayment for the cost of my upkeep."

Plainly, she expected disapproval from him, but he could not disapprove. Not ever. He'd disliked Clay from the moment he saw how little the man cared for Edith, and could not bear to think of her wondering why the man who stood in place of her father had no shred of kindness for her. "You did not deduct the cost of your labor?"

"I ought to have." She laughed, a sound of delight. His heart soared at the triumph of amusing her. "Louisa sent me a lovely note, though. She wished me all the best and hoped we would meet again one day. She is a well-bred young lady."

"Agreed."

"I love her for her generosity and friendship. Anyone would."

"I am glad you were not alone." There went his heart and his hopes again. Killed dead. Did she think she could persuade him to offer for Miss Louisa Clay?

She put a hand on his knee then snatched it away. "I'm sorry *you* were."

There was nothing he could say that was not dangerous. The carriage crossed the bridge into Hopewell-on-Lyft. The Duke's Arms would soon be on their left, then another wood and the hill to her home. The mail coach had just stopped at The Duke's Arms, and there was a deal of accompanying noise. When they were past, he lowered the glass.

"Why Hope Springs?" he asked. They were in the woods now, and he could not help watching the road for danger. This portion of the road, with the cover of dense trees and the approaching turn, was terrain a highwayman would find conducive to robbery. "Besides the legend of Robin Hood, that is."

"Who would not wish to live so near where Robin Hood and Maid Marian were lovers?"

"Who indeed."

She lifted a hand and, with a shrug, let it fall to the seat. "I asked my solicitor to find me properties in Nottinghamshire and, behold, Hope Springs was on the list and well within my budget. And I thought—"

The carriage shuddered to a stop. The coachman shouted, an inarticulate sound abruptly cut off.

They were not yet at Hope Springs.

"Stand and deliver!"

Oxthorpe reached under the seat for his pistol.

Chapter Ten

EDITH PUT A hand to her mouth and told herself not to panic. Nothing would be gained by that. The fact that Oxthorpe was sanguine helped. His mouth thinned, and there was something dreadful about his focus. From nowhere, he'd produced a pistol. Now that she saw it in his hands, it was as if the weapon were the only living thing in the carriage.

His coachman shouted, "Oi there, you poxy devil, do you know who you've stopped? The bloody duke himself."

Hope and denial both washed over her. A man must be desperate indeed to rob a duke.

Oxthorpe checked his pistol and murmured, "Don't be a fool, John Coachman."

Another voice replied, "A gentleman with a right deep pocket, I'll warrant."

The duke slid closer to the left-side door. "Remove what jewelry you cannot bear to lose, Edith. Leave the rest, or they'll know something is amiss and search the carriage." She removed a bracelet and the ebony hair combs that had belonged to her mother as quickly as she could. Her necklace and earrings must be sacrificed.

He tapped a panel at the far side of the carriage and exposed a hideyhole. She handed him what she'd removed. He traded the wallet in his pocket for the much-thinner one he took from inside then deposited her items and closed up the panel.

The carriage door opened on the side nearest her, and her heart slammed against her chest. Had the robbers seen what the duke had done?

Cold air rushed in. "My liege," the robber called out in a singsong voice. "Come stretch your legs, and take the air."

Oxthorpe surged forward, blocking the doorway. From behind him, she caught a glimpse of a lanky figure dressed in ill-fitting black clothes. The highwayman trained a pistol on the doorway. The duke was out of the carriage now, his own pistol held behind his back.

"Who have you got with you?" He waved the gun. "Let's have him out. Non-compliance means a shot through the heart. Come on, lad. Out with you."

Edith descended, frightened, yet reassured by the duke's calm demeanor. Still with his pistol concealed, Oxthorpe assisted her from the carriage.

Two men had stopped them. One trained a pistol on the coachman, who'd been made to dismount from the top seat of the carriage. The second highwayman had a youth's gangly, loose-limbed body, a boy primed to murder. An ill-fitting mask obscured his face. Early in his criminal apprenticeship, she thought.

The other robber was a more solid man. "Madam Duchess," this robber said. He did not waver in pointing his gun at the duke. "Your purse and your jewels. Empty your pockets, if you please."

One hard look from the duke stopped her from denying she was the Duchess of Oxthorpe. She did as she was told and divested herself of the jewelry she had retained. She also made a show of going through her pockets. "I haven't a purse, sir."

"What? No pin money of your own?"

She shook her head. How could the duke be calm at a time like this? Oxthorpe rested a hand on her shoulder. "My love," he said. "My dearest." She moved closer to the duke. "My wife is with child, sir. I beg you, allow her to return to the carriage."

She put her free hand on her stomach and willed herself to look as if that were so.

"We'll have your cloak and your slippers, too, ma'am."

"In this weather? This is an outrage." Oxthorpe took a step forward.

She did not have to pretend to be afraid. "No." She clutched his coat, though she knew enough not to interfere with whatever might come to pass with his weapon. "No, you mustn't."

"Duchess." His gaze lanced through her. He ordered—commanded—with that look. "Return to the carriage this moment."

The older robber was implacable. "Leave the cloak, if you please."

She divested herself of the garment and dropped it to the ground beside the other items. The younger one scooped up the smaller items and shoved them into his pockets.

"The carriage, my dear." Nothing betrayed Oxthorpe as anything but serene.

She complied, but her heart beat too fast, her hands shook, and her legs felt disconnected from her body. These ruffians had weapons, and even after they'd emptied their pockets, the duke had not been allowed to return to the carriage.

Once she was inside, Oxthorpe slammed the door shut. Through the glass, she saw him move forward, a lunge toward the gangly young highwayman. She hadn't expected him to be so fast. At the end of that motion, somehow, Oxthorpe had two pistols. He pointed one at the youth and the other at the older man.

Oxthorpe addressed the younger man. "Return my wife's possessions, if you please. Do not move, sir." He adjusted his aim when the other highwayman shifted. "Do you think I don't recognize your voices? The way you stand? You were brought before me at the quarter sessions eighteen months ago and plainly learned nothing from the experience."

The older man kept his hands lifted. "I'm the New Sheriff of Nottingham."

"The devil you are. Go home to your family, and pray God you are never again so stupid as to try your hand at highway robbery, for I promise, I shall have no mercy on you another time." He shifted the positions of both guns. "I'll see your backs or see you dead."

The gangly robber took off running.

"You." Oxthorpe sneered. He turned his full attention on the remaining man. "I don't want to see you before me again. You and your brother will hang if you continue in this fashion."

The other highwayman dashed into the trees, too, and it seemed an eternity to her that Oxthorpe sighted along the barrel of the pistol, tracking the man's progress through the trees. Any moment, she expected him to fire.

He didn't. He lowered his hand and stood for some moments, staring into the woods. In this new silence, the coachman gathered the remaining items on the ground, but he staggered when he straightened, and everything scattered once again. The duke looked at him. "John?"

"A mean knock on the head, Your Grace."

He nodded to the top of the carriage and handed one of the pistols to him. "Up then. I'll drive." He held up a hand and in clipped words said, "No argument."

Before Oxthorpe came to the door of the carriage, he retrieved all the items on the ground. He handed her their things and deposited his in a pile on the seat. He dropped the pistols into the pockets of his coat. "He's in no condition to drive, Edith."

"I understand."

"I'll have you home in no time." He secured the door, and a moment later, the carriage was headed uphill again. She could not afterward decide if it had taken a lifetime to reach Hope Springs or, as he'd promised, no time at all.

She was, she thought, perfectly fine. Entirely in control of herself while she walked to the door with the duke at her side. She had her bracelet and hair combs safely in her pocket. As he had the last time he walked with her to her door, he said nothing. This time, though, he stepped inside with her.

"Your Grace, I—" She put a hand over her mouth to stop the sob that rose in her chest. Her tidy, happy world had been severely shaken.

He was a duke. If she'd won a hundred and fifty thousand pounds she'd not be his social equal. That he was standing here in her house was a miracle of condescension. That he had called her his duchess and said she was with child—the invention of desperation, but my God. My God. He'd called her *my love* and *dearest*.

He put a hand on her shoulder. A light touch. "Shall I call your maid?"

Her heart was lead. So small and heavy. "You might have been killed."

A faint crease appeared between his eyes. "Your point?"

"That you might have been killed."

"So might you have."

"*I* did not confront two desperate highwaymen. Blackguards who could have murdered you."

"Neither one of them was the New Sheriff of Nottingham. In that respect, those two are imposters who ought to know better than to play at such games."

"That was no game. Or do you intend to argue no one's pistol was loaded?"

His expression turned fierce. "No."

"How do you know they aren't the ones robbing everyone left and right?"

"Allow me to represent to you that I recognized them instantly and that, further, I saw them at The Duke's Arms at the same time the actual New Sheriff robbed some other poor soul."

"Does it matter?" She could scarcely speak. "You could be dead now, and it would have been my fault. You were right. You've been right about everything. I ought to have left your boot in the field."

"I—"

"I ought to have refused to let you drive me home."

"Edith—"

The sound of her given name shocked her. He'd called her that before, when they were in the carriage and he was preparing to face death. He'd said her name the way a lover would. He could not possibly think that. *Edith.*

"Come here." He took her hands in his, and she walked forward as if he were anyone, an everyday person, anyone one might simply meet. He folded his arms around her, and she leaned against him.

There was a moment of awkwardness. In the back of her whirling thoughts, a voice warned her not to presume like this, but he drew her close, so close. His arms around her broke a barrier, demolished her defenses. His body was solid, and his heart beat steadily. She was racked. Shaken by what had happened, but far more by what could have happened.

"We might both be dead." She sniffed and breathed in his scent. "Lying there at the side of the road, bleeding. Gone."

"Darling." His low, soft whisper wound around her. "Where are your servants?"

Chapter Eleven

EDITH WALKED INTO the stationers accompanied by her maid. While Edith headed for the counter, her maid found a seat on a bench along one side of the shop. The proprietor leaned his forearms on the counter top. "Good day to you, miss."

"A good day to you, sir. Come now. You know why I am here. I have your note in my pocket."

"That I do, miss. That I do." He reached under the counter and brought out several sheets of paper.

"Oh. Lovely." She spread the paper out on the blotter that covered a portion of the counter. She had already purchased stationery printed with her name and direction at the top: *Miss Edith Clay, Hope Springs, Hopewell-on-Lyft, Nottinghamshire.* She'd even commissioned the design of a rose to be printed in red on every sheet. An extravagance that had been a fair trouble to have done to her satisfaction. This custom paper of hers was one of the expenses that leaped to the front of her mind whenever she fretted over having spent too much money.

And yet here she was because the stationer had sent her a note to the effect that he had just received shipments from Paris and Florence, and would she be interested in seeing them first? The sheets before her were samples for her examination.

"This is the Italian?" she asked.

"Yes, miss."

"Lovely." There was a blue cast to the paper she quite liked. She held up the other. Smooth grained, a fine, tight weave. "The French, I take it."

"Indeed." He set pen and ink on the counter. "Go ahead, miss. You'll not know if this is paper you want until you've written on it."

"Right you are. Thank you." She examined the pen. "You have one of the steel-nibbed pens."

"Newly arrived from London."

"Do you like it? It's not too rough on the paper?"

"I've not found it so. I have a quill, if you prefer."

"Oh no. I should like to try this." From the corner of her eye, she saw there was another customer. He'd been on the opposite side of the shop. She dipped the pen in the ink but froze when she realized it was the Duke of Oxthorpe and that he was making his way to her.

She held the pen suspended over the bottle. Somehow, this man who had never been anything to her but a title—words, a crest, a man whose existence was embodied in the word Oxthorpe—had become someone she knew well enough to expect they would greet each other. Remarkable. She, Miss Edith Clay, a woman of no consequence, was personally acquainted with a duke. "Your Grace."

She owed him her life.

The duke nodded in his curt way. "How do you do, Miss Clay?"

She tapped the nib of her pen against the rim of the inkwell and curtsied. "Well, thank you. May I hope the same for you?"

"Yes." He wore a green coat, buckskins, and the maroon boots. In one hand he held his hat, in the other, a notebook. His hair, medium length but thick and black, was cut short at the sides. She had an inappropriate urge to discover what it would be like to run her fingers through it.

He fell quiet, but she understood this was his way. He was not a talkative man. Once, she'd imagined him sitting alone in his house, a monster ready to devour anyone who came near. What she imagined now was a man who had both his rank and his natural reticence working against him.

She smiled at him. If he continued in his gruff ways the rest of his life, she would defend him to anyone. Anyone. "I very much like the notebooks sold here."

"Daykin & Towle make excellent paper." Daykin & Towle being the local papermaker.

"They do. I have laid in my supplies." She turned to the sheet of Italian paper and wrote her name across the top. "From time to time, however, I wish to write upon paper that speaks to me in a foreign language. I see myself now, sitting at my desk, dashing off the most amusing note on the finest Italian paper." She mimed writing. "My dearest Louisa, I had broiled smelt for breakfast. They were most excellent."

"*Affascinante.*"

She laughed, and the duke might actually have smiled, though one could never be certain. He was no troll beneath the bridge, not if he could laugh. She dipped her pen again and wrote quickly at the bottom of the sheet before her nerve abandoned her. "I am having a small party tomorrow evening. You ought to come. At six. Mr. Amblewise will be there. Mr. Jacobs is an astronomer from Bunney. I do not know if you have met him, but he has engaged to show us the stars if the night is clear."

"I know of him."

She wrote:

> Miss Edith Clay requests the honour of your presence at Hope Springs for dinner and stargazing, weather permitting.
> Thursday at 6:00 p.m.
> *Répondez, s'il vous plait.*

Underneath the last line, she drew a flourish and blotted the paper. She carefully folded and tore the sheet and handed the bottom portion to the duke. "There. I am sure you have obligations every hour of the day and night, but should you discover you are not otherwise engaged, I would be delighted to have you join my party."

He unfolded the sheet and examined the page gravely before he tucked it into an inside pocket of his coat. "I shall consult my schedule."

"*Grazie, Duc.*" He would never accept, of course, but she was glad to have made the effort. If he did not wish to make friends, that was his choice. But if he were to attend, he might find he had made one or two. They parted and went their separate ways, and Edith could not help feeling they might themselves one day be friends.

Later that afternoon, she was sitting down to tea when her butler brought her an envelope on a salver. But this was not the post. The letter, with its distinctive seal, was from Oxthorpe. She took the letter. "Thank you."

"There is a boy waiting outside, miss." He bowed and extended a second letter, this one intriguingly thick and also from Oxthorpe. "He's brought a gig and a horse he says are for you."

"A boy?" She opened the thicker of the letters, beyond curious at receiving not one but two letters from him. Inside this one were three folded sheets. The topmost was an invoice for the gig and necessary accoutrements, the second for the horse. The combined amount was enough to make her heart beat faster. She had the funds, she told herself. This purchase would not bankrupt her.

On the third sheet, he'd written two paragraphs, on paper with his crest embossed at the top. They informed her he was attaching the invoices and sending along one William Benedict, who, he had reason to believe, would make her an excellent groom, if she were of a mind to hire him.

She looked up. "Tell Mr. Benedict I shall be with him shortly."

"Yes, miss."

She slipped the other letter into her pocket, for this development required her time and attention. In far less precise letters at the bottom of the paragraphs, though it was plain the entire document was in the same hand, was the word *Oxthorpe*. Once, that word had conjured up a cold and forbidding feeling.

Outside, William Benedict stood beside the gig. A young man of seventeen or eighteen, tall and gangly, he snatched off his hat when she came down the stairs. He bowed. "Miss Clay."

He struck her as familiar, but she could not think where she'd seen him before. She walked around the gig. Gleaming black-lacquer body with a black leather seat and folded-down cover. The inside rims of the wheels were painted yellow, the spokes green. The duke's colors, which she supposed must be a coincidence. Perhaps the carriage maker did so for every vehicle the duke ordered. She ran a hand along the leather seat and the side of the gig.

"Are you from Hopewell-on-Lyft, Mr. Benedict?"

"No, miss." He watched her walk around to the horse. "From Bunney."

"I like his looks. Do you?" She patted the gelding's shoulder. It was dark gray with a black mane.

"I do, miss." He shifted his weight between his feet. "You'll have no trouble with him."

She considered the young man, and his familiarity to her was as coincidental as the colors of the gig's wheels. If Oxthorpe believed in this boy enough to send him to her, then she would not disagree. "His Grace recommends you highly. Do you know why?"

Benedict swallowed hard. "I'm grateful for the chance, miss. I work hard. I'm honest."

"So long as you want to earn an honest wage."

He swallowed again. "Yes, miss."

"Would you like to work for me?"

"I would, miss." His hands crushed the brim of his hat. In short order, they settled the details of what she would pay, his days off, that she expected to see him at church, and that she would pay for two suits for him to wear.

"You have no desire to supplement your income by any other means, I hope."

"No, miss. Thank you, miss." He met her gaze for only an instant before his focus skittered away, but his cheeks turned bright red.

"Go around to the back after you've seen to the gig and the horse, then. You'll be looked after."

"Thank you." He bobbed his head.

"You'll let me know if there's anything you need."

"I shall, miss."

She had a gig. A very smart gig among gigs. There could hold her head high when she attended the next meeting of the assembly committee. For that, she had the duke to thank.

It wasn't until two or three hours later that she remembered Oxthorpe's other letter. She left off writing to Louisa about her gig and the beauty of the horse that was new to her stables and drew the letter from her pocket. She bent the paper enough to lift the seal without badly breaking it. This must be instructions for remitting the monies she owed him. But it wasn't. It was his reply to her impromptu invitation to dinner, signed with his title. *Oxthorpe.*

Not his regrets.

An acceptance.

Chapter Twelve

WHAT IF NO one came? Edith jumped up from her seat in the drawing room and began pacing again. This was her first official dinner party at Hope Springs, and she was nervous about her guests and all that might go wrong. Dinner might be burned. She might spill something on her gown—she wore her best silk tonight, and her ebony hair combs, too, because she now considered them doubly lucky: because of her mother and, now, the duke.

She smoothed her skirt and told herself she would not consult the time again. She did, though. She'd had acceptances from them all but Mrs. Quinn and her husband, who had an engagement that night. The members of the assembly committee, naturally. Mr. Jacobs, the astronomer, and others.

What if her guests had been robbed on their way here? Whoever this New Sheriff of Nottingham was had robbed a gentleman on his way to Scotland just three days ago.

Outside, she heard a carriage arrive. Until her butler announced Mr. Thomas and his wife, she was convinced the arrival must be either a servant carrying regrets or the constable with terrible news of the fate of one of her guests.

Mrs. Thomas entered first, and Edith was beyond relieved for their safe arrival. Mr. Thomas met her with a hearty "Good evening," and a bow over her hand. His wife was all smiles and a quick kiss on the cheek.

"You had an uneventful drive, I hope?" Her encounter with the highwaymen had made her anxious about the safety of all her friends. Word of the duke's bravery had got out, not because he'd said anything, but because she'd told everyone who would listen.

"We did, Miss Clay." The former ambassador to the Porte briefly set a hand on her shoulder. "We made good time and met with no robbers."

Mrs. Thomas looped her arm through Edith's. "You've done wonders with this room."

She welcomed the distraction of the remark, no more because it was a heartfelt compliment. She was determined to surround herself with colors that she loved. "I was so worried the color would not be what I hoped, but it is precisely the shade of orange I wanted to have in this room."

"Perfection, if you ask me."

"Thank you." Mrs. Thomas had dressed in a reminder of her husband's former occupation, for she wore a turban and a gown of gold-and-blue silk brocade. A sash wound around her waist, and her slippers matched that band of silk. Her husband stood by his wife and beamed at her. "May I say what a lovely ensemble this is?" Edith said. "Wherever did you find such a fabric?"

"Anatolia. The souk in Aleppo. Mr. Thomas thought I'd gone mad, as much as I bought."

"No, no, not in the least." She gave the former diplomat a sideways smile. "No one would be mad to buy such gorgeous cloth as this. Why, to do so defines good sense and a rational mind."

"There, you see?" Mrs. Thomas sent her husband an arch and fond look. "*She* understands."

"Since you are divine in that gown, beloved wife, I cannot now disagree that you were correct when we were at the souk."

She blew him a kiss. "There was never a woman luckier in her husband than I."

"Nor I in my wife."

Edith wanted to sweep them both into a hug. They loved each other, and it brought both joy and tears to her heart to see that fondness.

The others arrived in short order. Distinguished and silver-haired Mr. Jacobs who, weather permitting, would lead their stargazing: Mrs. Bolingbase; Mr. Amblewise. Mr. Greene, a gifted artist, and his wife, and the Worthys. Mrs. Worthy, Edith had discovered, was pure inspiration at the pianoforte. No Oxthorpe as of yet, but since her receipt of his acceptance, she had decided that he would not, in fact, arrive. She'd given him the invitation too informally. His acceptance to her must have been sent in the same less-than-serious manner.

There was no reason for her to delay dinner. All the guests she'd expected to attend were present. Quite wisely, she'd not mentioned the possibility that the duke might attend. Their numbers for what she hoped would be a semiregular gathering were complete. She summoned a footman and gave instructions that dinner was to be served in twenty minutes.

Much sooner than she expected, her butler appeared in the doorway.

"Ah," she said to the others, turning away from the door. "Dinner is served."

Behind her, Walker cleared his throat. "His Grace, the Duke of Oxthorpe."

The astonishment that paralyzed her was reflected in the faces of her guests. Mr. Thomas stood at the sideboard with the wine he intended for his wife. Those guests who were seated rose. Edith turned and indeed, the duke was moving toward her. She blinked several times. He was here.

The duke took her hand. "Miss Clay."

"Duke." He was resplendent in a coat of midnight blue, a pewter waistcoat, and tan breeches. His much-traveled top boots were a divine complement to his attire. A sapphire gleamed from a ring on his index finger.

With a smile that was nearly friendly, he greeted those guests whom he already knew. She introduced him to the guests to whom he had not yet been introduced. After a brief, awkward silence as they adjusted to his unexpected arrival and the impact of his considerable presence, Mrs. Thomas filled in the conversation. Yes. Yes, indeed, she was the wife of a diplomat. Mrs. Worthy was of great assistance, too, in overcoming the difficulties. She was a delightful and attractive woman who did not quail when the duke turned his pale eyes on her.

Imagined difficulties never emerged. Oxthorpe was not a man of many words, but neither was he the silent figure she'd feared he might be. His erudition shone through, and he listened attentively to the others when they spoke. He was charming in his quiet way, both interested and interesting. She did not think she was the only one to notice that he and Mrs. Worthy got on well, and it was a rare woman who managed that feat.

After dinner, they gathered again in the drawing room. Mr. Greene, who lived on the other side of the Lyft, picked up pencil and paper and sketched likenesses with his usual uncanny deftness, much to everyone's delight and appreciation.

"Tell me, Mr. Greene," Mr. Thomas said, "will you be at the assembly to dance with our Miss Clay?"

Still sketching, he glanced up from his sheet of paper long enough to wink at Edith. "Wouldn't miss it for the world."

"Did they not just have an assembly?" the duke asked. At the moment, he was sitting by the fire, holding a glass of French burgundy that had come very dear. She had her own glass, as she refused to restrict the ladies to sherry. The vintage was worth every penny she'd paid to stock her cellar.

"You are thinking of last quarter, Your Grace." Mrs. Thomas peeked at Mr. Greene's work. "That's quite good."

"Thank you." Greene used a finger to smudge a line.

"The first Monday of every quarter."

Oxthorpe tilted his head. "Not this quarter, though. Is not the Christmas assembly to take place on the twenty-second?"

"Yes. Our holiday assembly is rightly famous, and the closer it is to the holiday, why, the better, Your Grace." Mrs. Thomas curtsied to the duke. "Thanks to generous gifts of benefactors such as Miss Clay and yourself. This year's Christmas assembly will be especially grand."

"Have no fear," Mr. Greene said, "I shall be there. Indeed, I cannot imagine a pleasanter way to spend an evening than dancing with Miss Clay and the other young ladies of Hopewell-on-Lyft and environs."

Oxthorpe nodded as if he were responsible for organizing the entire event. "I hope the young ladies and gentlemen of the town enjoy the gathering."

"We would be so pleased if you attended." Mrs. Thomas moved away from Mr. Greene and walked along the short side of the wall.

"I have a great many obligations."

"Yes, yes. You are traveling to Northumberland. You did tell me that. I'd forgotten."

Edith noted he did not correct Mrs. Thomas's supposition. Was he going after all, then?

And so the evening went. Moving from one subject to another, and each of them contributing. They were not, alas, able to stargaze, as the clear sky of earlier in the day had given way to clouds. There was not a star to be seen.

Oxthorpe made his good-byes at a quarter past eleven, and by half 'til midnight she was bidding good night to the last of her guests. Soon after, she told her staff to retire, for they'd made quick work of clearing the parlor and the dining room. The rest could be seen to in the morning.

She walked through the house and experienced one of those moments of still, quiet joy. She, Miss Edith Clay, once penniless and with a future of nothing but dependence, had given a dinner party all on her own. With her friends and acquaintances. The Duke of Oxthorpe had been in attendance, in her home. Hers. She headed for the stairs, but when she reached them, she did not go up. Instead, she drew her shawl about her shoulders and walked into her garden, never mind the incipient chill of winter.

As times like this, she was so grateful for the change in her circumstances she could scarcely contain her emotions. She tipped her head back to see the sky. The night had been too cloudy for stargazing, though now a few stars sparkled through the areas where the clouds had thinned. There was no moon to speak of, covered as it was by clouds, but there was light from the house.

"Miss Clay?"

She turned in the direction of the gate that led to the stable. "I thought you'd gone home."

"I misplaced Mr. Greene's sketch of me." The duke reached over to unfasten the gate. He crossed the lawn and joined her on her flagstone terrace.

"You needn't have gone to the trouble of returning when you might have sent a servant."

"I hadn't got far."

"Manifestly." He unsettled her because he was an object of magnificent terror. "You make that complaint of me so often. I cannot pass by the chance to address your favorite admonition to you."

"Fair enough."

"In addition, Duke, it is cold."

He chuckled. "Then why, one wonders, are you outside, Miss Clay? You ought to be inside sitting before the fire."

"I shall be. Soon." She faced the house.

"What?"

She glanced at him, and there was enough light for her to make out his face, but not the details of his expression. "This is my house."

"It is indeed."

"I own it, free and clear, and I have money enough that I need not worry about the yearly taxes."

He took off his hat. "Not your cousin's."

"Not a single brick. It's miraculous."

"A good Nottinghamshire house often is."

She could not help a smile. "The very best county in which to own a house."

"I am glad to have had the chance to dine here. On dishes that match my eyes."

"Your Grace, one of these days, someone is going to realize you have a piquant sense of humor."

"You've kept my secret so far."

He'd come close, a head taller than she, and though it was too dark to make out any details of his expression, she knew what he looked like. He put his hands on either side of her face, gently pressing his palms to her cheeks.

She put a hand over one of his. The side of her finger brushed over the ring he wore. "Such warm hands."

His silence was comfortable now. She understood him better, knew this was simply his way. He moved closer, and that was a barrier crossed that made her breath catch.

"Edith."

Inside the house, the case clock in the rear parlor began its midnight chime. "This is not wise."

At the last chime of the clock, soft and distant, the duke bent his head to hers. "I don't care."

Her stomach took flight. He was going to kiss her. He was. He might.

The silence stretched out.

Please. Please, please.

"Go inside, Miss Clay. I would be devastated if you took a chill."

Chapter Thirteen

OXTHORPE SET HIS mare away from his hunting box on the vale side of Killhope Castle. He'd had good hunting yesterday, two stags sent back with his gamekeeper earlier this morning. He emerged from the woods into a gap that overlooked the Vale of West. To his right, the Lyft glittered with the morning sun. The canal and locks that would take a boater into Hopewell-on-Lyft were well behind him, on the complete other side of the castle. Ahead lay the stream that fed the pond between his property and Hope Springs, not yet frozen, though there would surely be a layer of ice.

The snow on the ridge was melting. Only the ground still in shadow remained white. The vale below glittered with frost. Before long, the vale, too, would be white with snow.

The three days of respite he'd promised himself were at an end, but he'd been tempted to extend his stay. Alas, he was due in Nottingham tomorrow afternoon. He had made an appointment with Mr. Madison some days ago so as to have an excuse to be away for that damned assembly. He urged his horse forward. A part of him was infernally aware of how close he was to the boundary with Hope Springs. Not a quarter mile distant. Less.

When, tomorrow morning, it became known he'd left Killhope, she'd think he was on his way to Holmrook to propose to Louisa. And she'd be pleased. Not devastated. No, she'd be devastated when he returned unencumbered by an engagement.

His horse continued along the path that led to the uppermost boundary line. For some fifty yards, this path demarked the two properties. Had it been his great-grandfather who had married the woman who'd brought that property into the Fletcher family holdings?

In the distance, he could see the pond and the hill that obscured a straight view to Hope Springs. More distant yet was the forest between Hopewell-on-Lyft and Hope Springs, traversed by the Great Northern Road. As he approached a curve in the path, he heard someone on the path ahead of him.

His gamekeeper? Not possible since the man was on his way to Killhope with the venison and birds he'd taken. Mr. Amblewise, perhaps, if he was traveling between parishioners. Or the New Sheriff of Nottingham.

No sense taking chances. Before he rode around the corner, he checked the pistol in his pocket and kept it at the ready.

Not a servant, nor the vicar, nor a robber, but Edith. She stood at the edge of the path, the reins to a tall bay mare clenched in one hand, her whip in the other. Edith was not, as he had previously observed, an accomplished horsewoman. The horse was perhaps not the most suitable mount for a woman who was not confident in her abilities.

No wonder she'd been so worried about the purchase of another when she had bought, or more accurately, been sold a headstrong animal that did not suit her. Her groom was nowhere to be seen.

With a cheerful grin, she lifted her whip hand in greeting. "Good morning, Your Grace."

"Miss Clay." Not one word exchanged between them since he'd come so perilously close to kissing her. Not a word. He'd not dared take the liberty. His emotions rode too near to the surface with her.

"Lovely morning." She wore a green habit and a matching hat with black feathers. Her boots, too, were green.

"Where is your groom?"

"On his way back to Hope Springs. His horse threw a shoe."

"You did not accompany him?"

"I meant to. But she"—she nodded at her horse—"preferred otherwise. I don't know what's got into her. She's not usually this much trouble. Then I dismounted, and, well, you see the predicament I am in."

Indeed, he did. Unless she found a stump or a rock to stand on, she would not be able to remount that mare on her own. "Shall I assist you?"

Her relief touched him. "Thank you, yes. I was resigned to walking home."

"No need for that." He dismounted and joined her. He bent, hands cupped. She put her foot on his hands, he boosted her up, and she swung into her saddle, and that was that.

He remounted. "I shall ride with you." With some effort, he gentled his voice. "If that would be agreeable."

"How kind. Thank you."

He did not move. Neither did she. She adjusted her skirts, an endeavor that included—deliberately or by coincidence—her averting her gaze from him. He could not think what to say to her. The silence killed him. Crushed him. Desperation sent words from his brain to his mouth with no stop in between for reflection. "Did your bouquets of mistletoe pass muster with the assembly committee?"

"They did. We have been madly tying ribbons and lace ever since."

That night, he thought he'd saved himself from a mistake, and now, he saw, he hadn't. Not at all. He could not bear the thought of having lost what little progress he'd made with her, yet he had. He had. "I regret I shan't be there to see them."

As he'd known, this brought a smile to her face. "Oh?"

"I have business to attend to."

"In Northumberland?"

He crushed her hopes, too. "In Nottingham." Another silence descended. Defeated, he nodded in the other direction. Away from Hope Springs. Toward Killhope. "This way, then."

"Hope Springs is that way." She pointed.

"There is a view," he said. "You will admire it." A command. All wrong. He meant for her to hear that he wanted her to see the view, but no. By habit, he demanded that she accompany him. "I should like for you to see it. Please."

She nodded. Whatever she thought privately of his peremptory manner, they rode in companionable quiet to the top of the ridge with its view of the Vale of West and the towers of Killhope Castle.

She leaned forward, and he saw the view with new eyes, hers. "This, sir, is why I chose to live in Nottinghamshire. Surely there is nowhere else in England so lovely as this."

"None."

Her gaze stayed on him. "Thank you, Your Grace, for sending William to me."

"I hope he gives satisfaction."

"I shall do my best to deserve your trust in me." She looked out over the vale again. "The gig is everything I wished. Thank you. I hope you received my cheque for the amount."

"Promptly." He let as many minutes pass as he could stand before he directed his horse along the path that would, as it happened, take them past his hunting box. She followed, and that he must take as a positive sign. If she could but forgive him that awkwardness at Hope Springs, he would be grateful.

"This is one of the prettier rides on Killhope lands." In deference to her lack of skill in the saddle, he kept his horse to a walk.

"It is lovely here."

They rode side by side on a path that wound through trees and past a meadow still covered in a dusting of snow. He would have passed by his hunting box, but she stopped at the top of the tree-lined drive, gazing curiously toward the building.

"I'd no idea this was here. Who lives here?"

"I do. When I am hunting." This time, he filled the quiet before it was unendurable. "Would you care for a tour?" He braced himself for a polite no.

"Yes, thank you."

At the end of the driveway, he dismounted and held out a hand to assist her down. "None of the staff is here. I closed up the house this morning."

"Is this where you've been?" At his inquiring look, her cheeks turned pink. She was still on her horse, her hand reaching for his. "It was remarked you were not at home these past days. We thought you'd gone to London."

He knew what she would say next.

"Or Northumberland."

"I was here. Hunting." He moved in, close enough to set a hand on her waist if need be, but she slid off without incident. She put her wrist through the loop that held up the long skirt of her habit, and they walked to the stable. She waited by the doorway while he settled their horses.

On their way to the house by way of the back garden and the path to the front door, she looked avidly at the grounds. He said, "If it were spring, there would be more to admire here."

"I like this well enough." He put a hand to the back of her arm. Edith ignored her reaction to that. "Did your hunting go well?"

"Two bucks. A doe. When they are dressed, I shall send you a haunch. A pheasant as well, if you like."

"You are too kind. Thank you. What a Christmas dinner we shall have at Hope Springs with a goose, a pheasant, and venison."

He opened the front door for her and again had the odd experience of seeing the house as if it were new to him instead of familiar. As if he'd not spent the last three days here. He was not surprised that she walked first to what, at Killhope, would be the great hall. Here, a series of arched windows overlooked the woods only he had the right to hunt.

She went straight to the bow windows. There was a window seat, but she stood to the side, inches from the glass, one hand on the carved stone that separated the window casings. When he joined her, not too close, she turned. At ease because she did not see him with intimate eyes. Nothing at all like the way he saw her. "You think you don't notice, but you're wrong."

"About?"

"This. This lovely little house, and the panorama before us. Beauty like this becomes a part of one's heart and soul."

"It does."

"I've felt it happening to me since I came to Hope Springs."

"It is a pretty property."

"It is. You've shown me Killhope and your conservatory. That view. And now this." She whirled to the window again and spread her arms wide. "This, too, is a part of me."

He came to where she stood and sat on the window seat, arms crossed, legs stretched out. "I would say come here when you like, but this is no fit place for a lady."

She laughed, and the sound pierced his heart. "Can you imagine? You'd come here to hunt with all your gentlemen friends and acquaintances—"

"More likely only me."

"Even worse." She stared out the windows again, smiling. "You would say, 'Who has been sitting in my chair?'" She looked at the ceiling, laughing now.

He did not see how he could live without her. How could he bring himself to marry another woman when she owned his heart? Yet he must. He must. He could not remain unmarried, with no heirs. No sons. No children at all.

"You'd say, 'Who has been eating in my dining room and sleeping in my bed?' Then you would find a snoring lump on your chaise—"

"A chaise-longue, here? I think not."

She glanced around. There was little furniture, but chairs for servants or people asked to wait on his pleasure. A table or two against the wall. A carpet from India covered most of the floor here. "Very well, your favorite armchair, my shoes on the floor, my shawl fallen to the ground, and me, insensible from the beauty of the view."

She showed no awareness that she had said something one might take as meaning more than the mere words. Something salacious. Because she had not intended any such thing. Yet. Yet he could not dismiss the idea. Of her in his bed.

She cocked her head. The ribbon tied beneath her chin glinted dully in the light. "Have I said something wrong?"

"No."

"I have." She stepped closer. "You are the most inscrutable man I have ever met."

He laughed. No mirth at all.

"I'm quite serious." She studied him. "No." Her quiet voice lanced through him. "Don't look away. Not when I am about to understand you."

"Are you certain you wish to?" He held her gaze, and the silence of his hunting box became unendurable. He fixed in his head an image of her in his bed. Nude. And of him, there to touch, and taste, experiencing that moment when his prick slid into her body. Her. Not any woman, but her. Specifically. The woman who made him see beauty where he'd once seen only duty.

She blinked, and her cheeks turned pink. She did not look away from him. Nor did he look away from her. Then she did glance away, but her attention came back immediately. He was too much aware of the difference in their ranks. She was a lady, one could not deny her that, but though she'd lived with relatives who had rank and property, she was herself without distinction, born to no fortune, in the care of a relative whose neglect of her told the world the value he placed on her.

She had no pretensions. None at all. In London, she had never put herself forward. She did nothing to anger her cousin, yet she'd been unfailingly a friend to Miss Louisa Clay. Her champion in all things. She struck to his center, to his heart. Found him out. Assessed.

"Do you think no one could love you?" she asked.

"I do not think that."

She tilted her head again, then again, eyes narrowed while she stared into his soul. "You do. But why? Why would you think such a thing?"

"I've no illusions I am well liked."

"One does not simply *like* a duke." She stripped off her gloves and set them on the portion of the window seat that he did not occupy, and his heart raced away. "Dukes are terrifying personages."

He took one of her hands in his. "I terrify you."

"Naturally."

"How easily you say that." What would happen to him if this did not end where he hoped?

"I would be a most unusual woman if you did not." With her free hand, she traced three fingers along the line of his cheek, the underside of his mouth.

"Are you this moment?"

"I have never been more terrified of anyone than I am of you this moment."

He released her, spread his arms wide, and leaned back. "Go then, if you are in terror."

She stepped toward him, and for him the world disappeared, but for her. She freed her wrist from the loop of her habit and ran her fingers lightly through his hair, brushing it back and smoothing it down. Both hands. "Does your hair never lie flat?"

"Never." He set a hand on the back of her waist. He took and then let out a breath. "Edith." She left her hands on his head. He drew her closer and whispered, "I have never, ever forgotten you."

Her eyes fluttered. "You said that before."

"I did."

"What am I to make of that?"

"That it is true." He brought her toward him, and there was no denying at all that they had crossed another barrier. "I met you and never could think of any woman but you afterward."

"That can't be so."

"It is. I can't forget you. I never shall." The air trembled with awareness. "Another truth, Edith. I have never made love to a woman."

"No." Her eyes opened wide. "No, I don't believe that. I won't."

He removed her hat and stretched to set it on a nearby table. Having done that, he brought her back into his embrace. "I'm no innocent, you understand that, I hope."

She ran a hand over his head again, and then she leaned in and brushed her mouth over his.

Chapter Fourteen

CURIOSITY HAD SEPARATED her from good sense. Curiosity and a powerful longing to touch him. If they hadn't been so close, he with an arm around her and she with her hands in his thick, soft hair—not at all coarse, as she'd wondered—she wouldn't have dared. Plainly, quite plainly, he'd thought about this, too, or they'd not have ended up with her near enough to him to have touched his mouth with hers.

And?

And nothing.

He did nothing.

She put a hand to his chest and tipped her head back, waiting for the humiliation to pass, settling in herself the fact that she had misjudged their situation and his words. She tilted her head down, staring at the green fabric of her bodice, then at her fingertips on his breast. She would have to look at him. Not yet. Not yet.

His palm pressed against the small of her back. Deliberate, since she felt the flex of his biceps. She looked at him, and his eyes locked with hers, and she could not breathe for the need she saw there. A thousand thoughts flashed through his eyes, and he kept them all to himself. She had never known such a self-contained man, so few words and now none when she desperately needed them from him. His arms remained around her still.

She said, "Tell me if you want me to kiss you again, or if we must agree it did not happen. Tell me that much."

"Again, Edith."

She did. She leaned in again and kissed him, another light touch of her lips to his, before she drew away. "Like that?"

He shook his head. That was almost a smile. Almost.

"What could you mean, I wonder." She wound her hand around the back of his neck, above the collar of his coat. The world changed. Everything different. Everything new. Magical. She kissed him again. She smelled the outdoors. Him.

His arms were around her, his mouth under hers. More than a slide across his lips this time. At the last minute, his lower lip caught hers, and her life changed forever. Again.

Her body tingled, her chest tightened, she could not feel her knees. This was no game. No harmless flirtation. She went taut with need. She melted against him, tipped her head to his, and pressed her mouth against his. She kissed him, and he kissed her back, and she could not get enough of this ascension of her body into longing.

Had she really thought he would be as controlled in kissing as he was in everything else? How could she have? He cupped the back of her head, and she opened her mouth. She'd only ever kissed one other man. One lover. One devastation of her heart, and then Oxthorpe kissed her back. Not a game. Not something to be indulged and forgotten.

There was no mistaking his physical state, and they froze, the two of them, when she brushed a hand across the middle of the buttons on the left side of his breeches. He drew breath, and she saw His Grace, the Duke of Oxthorpe, who kept his silence, whom almost no one spoke of in terms of the qualities she knew he possessed. He was Oxthorpe, and the ability to say one knew him was the same as laying claim to power and influence.

He knew this. He knew and did not offer himself easily to anyone. He knew if he made his interest in a woman known that she might agree to anything. This, to a man like him, must be a fell power. How could anyone say no to Oxthorpe? The miracle, the miracle was that he'd not become a man who took every part of that power as his due.

Again, she brushed a finger along the fall of his breeches and decided against words. No words for now. She unfastened one of those leftmost buttons, then another, then her fingers were sliding inside, between fabric, linen. No games. Just her growing need and the leap of tension between them.

He brought her toward him, his body shifting, pulled up handfuls of her habit, and she moved with him, and the only thought in her mind was that he was going to put his cock inside her, fill her, and that was the miracle, that they could find each other like this.

His hands slid underneath her clothes then up to grip her bottom, and her life depended on balancing like this, on the spread of his thighs, on his lifting her up and positioning himself. She did the same, made the necessary adjustments, and when he pushed inside her, she met that motion with a shiver of her entire being toward bliss.

A moan left her, unadulterated bliss, because his sex in her was beyond perfect, the way her body accepted him, took him greedily. Already she was slipping away. She bit her lower lip and concentrated on what she was feeling. The pressure of him inside her, the strength of his arms around her, the scent of him, the way his expression changed with each push inside her, each answering roll and thrust from him.

His hands on her bottom brought her forward then relaxed, and she could feel the tension in his arms and legs, and she forgot she'd meant to be silent, for she gripped his shoulders, and put her mouth by his ear and said, "I wish I was naked. I wish you could touch me everywhere."

He thrust up. "Yes?"

"Yes, please, like that." She licked the outside of his ear. "I wish you were naked, too. I wish I could touch you and see all of you."

"You've seen me naked."

With a slow rock of her hips timed with his and restricted by the fact they were sitting, balanced indelicately and mostly by dint of his strength and willingness to be uncomfortable, rather than in a bed, she said, "I did not see enough."

He held her still, lips twitching. "If I'd walked out of the pond, you'd not have been appalled?"

"I would have been, but if I'd known this—"

"Edith—"

"If I'd known this about you, I would have walked to the shore and pulled you from the water."

He held her tight, fingers pressing her toward him. "You drive me mad."

"I wish I could see your parts." She kissed the side of his jaw, and his skin felt smooth, and she found a place where his pulse beat, and she kissed him there, too. "I wish I could see right now, this moment."

He tipped his shoulders back, pushed farther back into the window seat, setting one shoulder against the side of the window to brace himself. "I always oblige a lady."

"No, no." She shifted and found an angle that sent him deeper. Her arousal, the angle of his penetration made words an inconvenience, and yet the feelings in her were too big to keep to herself. She concentrated to find the words. "No, Oxthorpe. No." She grabbed either side of his face. "Stay, or I'll never forgive you."

"I'll not disappoint, then." His words ended in a low growl, and she watched his eyes close, the shift of his focus to the physical, to the contact between them, more, more than that, to his contact with her body, and she was fiercely glad of the sight. They were wordless now, reduced to inarticulate sounds.

The moment came when she was nothing but a reach for her approaching pleasure, and Oxthorpe, he wrapped an arm around her hips and pulled her close while his other hand worked beneath her skirts. His fingers stroked her, and she slipped away from everything but sensation.

Oxthorpe whispered, "Yes, my love. Yes."

She registered the sound, the satisfaction in those words, and then there were tears welling up along with her climax because such intense physical pleasure was not endurable. His fingers, the strokes of his fingers, and his cock moving in her, the reaction that caused annihilated her.

Chapter Fifteen

WITH A SINKING heart, Oxthorpe stood in front of the dark and empty parish hall. He must have mistaken the date of the assembly. It must have been Saturday, while he was still in Nottingham, cursing himself for wanting to send his regrets to Madison, at whose home he'd been invited to dine. Or perhaps Friday. It couldn't have been Sunday when he'd gone to church with Madison and then stayed at his hotel, telling himself he would not leave before his business was concluded Tuesday.

And then he had. He'd suffered through every appointment he'd made, interminable reviews of documents, and then dined with the actual Sheriff of Nottingham and left early. He'd left his valet at the hotel to arrange their return. He'd sent his regrets to Madison and left for Hopewell-on-Lyft. For nothing. All his hurrying and driving like a madman for nothing. His distraction and rudeness to Madison, with a steadily diminishing portion of his mind on business, and the bloody building hadn't a soul in it.

"Your Grace?"

He said nothing in response to his coachman's inquiry. He'd gone home first to change from traveling clothes to evening clothes, and now either he was too late, or he was here on the wrong day. All this commotion and disruption of his schedule, his heart entirely overtaken, and he'd come here on the wrong day?

"The roof is leaking again, Your Grace. They've moved the assembly to Carrington Close."

Slowly, he turned. "How do you know?"

The moon came out from behind the clouds, and he had a silvered view of his servant, bundled in scarfs, a thick coat, and gloves. With one heavy boot propped up, his coachman shrugged. He felt a pang of regret for keeping the man from the festivities. He must have wanted to attend. He'd given most of his staff at Killhope leave to attend. "That's what they did last year."

"Very well then." He kept his expression sober. Killhope had been quiet, not because it was late but because all but a skeleton staff had been there. All the rest were at the assembly. "To Carrington Close."

"Aye, Your Grace."

He strode back to the carriage and closed the door more loudly than was necessary. It would be thirty minutes, longer given it was cold and dark and icy, before he arrived anywhere near Edith. At this rate, he'd get there only to find everyone on their way home. Nothing but servants cleaning up the detritus of a party hastily relocated. If he'd known, if he'd been home when the parish hall roof sprang a leak, he could have offered up Killhope as a location.

Carrington Close was not dark. The windows blazed with lights, and a groom promptly came out to meet his carriage. His heart settled. Outside, he gave the groom a coin and called up to the coachman, "You'll come in for food and dancing, then?"

"Your Grace."

Oxthorpe took the front stairs two at a time. A wreath of pine and holly hung on the front door, festooned with a bow of blue ribbon and gold lace—Edith's work, he was certain. Inside, handed over his hat, scarf, and greatcoat and paid no attention to the glass of cider Mrs. Carrington's butler had hidden behind an urn.

At the door to the ballroom, he straightened the lay of his coat over his shoulders, tugged on his collar, smoothed his neckcloth. Another enormous wreath hung above the door, and there were blue ribbons and lace, and sprigs of holly all around the doorframe.

Inside, the music ended. The noise of the assembly reduced. Now, then. With a nod and a coin pressed into the waiting footman's hand, he walked into the ballroom as he should have every year the citizens of Hopewell-on-Lyft gave the party that brought them together in good cheer and spirits.

The footman rapped his staff on the floor loudly enough to cut through the noise. "His Grace, the Duke of Oxthorpe."

The lull in conversation died away to silence.

Wreaths and ribbons festooned the room. The mistletoe Edith had worked so hard to gather and decorate hung from every chandelier, sconce, or convenient beam.

Mrs. Carrington approached him with a pretty young woman at his side. Two of the ladies of the assembly committee followed her. Edith was not among them.

He would do this. Whether she was here or not, he would. The point was that he would not close himself off in solitude. Mrs. Carrington reached him first and sank into a curtsy. The young woman beside her curtsied as well. "Your Grace. You honor us with your presence."

"Not at all."

"Robina, may I introduce the duke?"

"I should be delighted."

"Miss Weston, the Duke of Oxthorpe. If you recall, I pointed out to you his home of Killhope Castle."

"Your Grace."

He smiled at Miss Weston, aware that he'd startled Mrs. Carrington. "You are the young lady who has been visiting Mrs. Herbert."

"Yes, Your Grace."

He was determined to make himself agreeable, and if that meant he astonished the good people of Hopewell-on-Lyft, so be it. "I hope you have been enjoying your stay in our village."

"Very much so."

"You must come to Killhope Castle for a tour."

"Thank you. I would like that very much, sir."

The other ladies of the committee reached him, and he greeted them in turn and accepted their exclamations of delight at his appearance. Alas, amid the decorations and tables laden with food and drink, the faces that gazed at him were not smiling because he was here. His arrival had made everyone tense. Did they think he would demand that they cease their merriment immediately? He wanted to do something that would astound everyone, something that would prove to Edith there was hope for him.

"Miss Weston." He sketched a bow to her. "You'll dance with me."

She managed to cover her astonishment. "I should love that, thank you."

He gave her a brilliant smile. Incandescent, he felt, and since, just then, the orchestra began the opening strains of another set, he held out his hand and waited for the very pretty Miss Weston to put her hand on his.

They danced, and she was a charming partner. Delightful. He ignored the stares and concentrated on amusing Miss Weston, and thank God, thank the Lord in Heaven, that he had asked her to dance and not some other young lady with less self-possession than Miss Weston.

Presently, though, their dance was over. It was, he discovered, the last set before the orchestra broke to have something to eat and drink and for the others to do the same. He walked Miss Weston to the side of the room. They passed Mr. and Mrs. Wattles, and he stopped to bid them good evening. His mood lightened. He was often at The Duke's Arms, doing custom with the Wattleses, and who would not admire the industry of a man who brewed an excellent beer in his cellar?

He and Miss Weston spent some minutes in conversation while they were in queue for cider, quite welcome on a cold winter evening. Everyone stood aside for him, though, and there he and Miss Weston were at the head of the line. Someone called out, "The mistletoe!"

He glanced up and indeed Miss Weston was standing directly beneath the mistletoe. They exchanged a look and, thank God, she was no more dazzled than Edith had ever been. Not in the least. He stepped toward her, took a berry from the bunch and kissed her. A short kiss. A kiss that was nothing but the good cheer of a Christmas assembly where people gathered to enjoy each other's company and exchange wishes for the holidays.

When he stepped back, amid much clapping, she gave him a curtsy and a warm smile, and there. Everyone would see he was not an ogre come to spoil their fete. "Your Grace."

"Miss Weston." He stepped past her and accepted a cup of cider from the footman to give to her, and then another for himself. By the time he turned around, Miss Weston had gone.

But there was Mr. Thomas with Goodman, too. He hurried to join them when he saw Miss Amanda Houston, a buxom brunette with a fine opinion of herself, heading toward him. Purple plumes in her hat bobbed as she walked. He found Miss Houston difficult to endure for long, for she had no appreciation for brevity and more than half a mind to one day be a duchess.

Goodman and Mr. Thomas greeted him heartily and closed ranks. He did not see Edith anywhere. It did not matter. She was right. He was too much alone, he shared too little, he accepted too little of the goodwill of the denizens of Hopewell-on-Lyft.

Mr. Amblewise and the blacksmith joined them. He listened while he ate two excellent pasties. Mr. Thomas told an amusing tale from his time in Anatolia, of the monkey that had escaped into his house in the section of Pera where foreign diplomats to the High Porte lived.

Across the room, he caught a glimpse of his coachman with a cup of punch. He and Edith's butler broke into an impromptu carol. One a tenor, one basso. Others joined in the song as someone tapped out the beat. While he dealt with the unwelcome emotion of the moment, Edith came in one of the side doors.

Edith.

To the background of the song, he walked across the ballroom floor, empty of dancers at the moment. "Edith."

She curtsied, and he took both her hands in his, and she broke into a grin that would have won his heart if she had not already had it. Her fingers tightened around his. She squeezed her eyes shut and then opened them again. "Your Grace. I thought you'd gone to Holmrook after all."

"I told you more than once I would not go. That I would be in Nottingham."

"But you left, and Mr. Clay invited you, and who would go to Nottingham for so many days at Christmas?"

"A fool."

"You're no fool." Her eyes were bright with tears, and she used the side of a gloved finger to wick away the damp. "Don't say that you are."

"No, I am not."

"I thought you'd gone."

He drew her close to him, and if those nearby saw them, he did not care. "Never. I never would." He brought her far too close for good manners. "Edith."

"What is it?"

"Edith, you are standing under mistletoe."

"I am?"

He pointed up.

She looked, and she smiled slowly. "So I am."

He kept his arms around her waist. There was a time for words, and this was one. "Marry me, Edith. Marry me, and I shall be the happiest man there ever was. Marry me, and I promise to spend my life making you happy. Marry me because I love you, and I do not want to imagine a life where I am not with you."

She blinked several times. "You love me?"

"Yes."

"I thought you did not care for me. You made me love you, and I thought you did not care for me the way I do for you."

"You were wrong."

She threw herself at him, arms tight around his shoulders. "Do you mean it? Do you really?"

"Darling," he whispered. "Darling Edith."

She stepped back and touched his cheek. "While you were gone, I realized I love you. I fell in love with you, and I was never so miserable in all my life than while I thought you'd gone to offer for Louisa."

"Marry me, Edith. I'll never be whole if you don't."

"Nor will I," she whispered.

"That is no answer."

Her smile warmed his soul. "Yes," she said. "Yes, a thousand times yes."

He drew her into his arms, and he kissed her. Not the polite kiss he'd given Miss Weston. This kiss was passion, and joy, and desire, and when he drew back, he looked into her eyes and she rested her head on his chest, and only then did he realize everyone was clapping. The entire room.

With Edith at his side, he returned to Thomas and Goodman, and others whom he must make his friends. He lifted his cider to the room at large and raised his voice. "My deepest, most sincere wishes for a holiday where we are surrounded by those we love, by the remembrance of those whom we have loved, and that we resolve we shall be men and women worthy of love. Merry Christmas to all!"

About Carolyn Jewel

Carolyn Jewel was born on a moonless night. That darkness was seared into her soul and she became an award-winning and USA Today bestselling author of historical and paranormal romance. She has a very dusty car and a Master's degree in English that proves useful at the oddest times. An avid fan of fine chocolate, finer heroines, Bollywood films, and heroism in all forms, she has two cats and two dogs. Also a son. One of the cats is his.

Visit Carolyn on the web at:

carolynjewel.com

Twitter: @cjewel

Facebook: facebook.com/carolynjewelauthor

Goodreads: goodreads.com/cjewel

Sign up for Carolyn's **newsletter** (http://cjewel.me/newsletter31) so you never miss a new book and get exclusive, subscriber-only content.

Excerpts

LORD RUIN
CHAPTER 1

London, 1818

CYNSSYR GLARED AT the door to number twenty-four Portman Square. "Blast it," he said to the groom who held two other horses. "What the devil is taking them so long?" He sat his horse with authority, a man in command of himself and his world. His buckskins fit close over lean thighs, and the exacting cut of his jacket declared a tailor of some talent. A Pink of the Ton, he seemed, but for eyes that observed more than they revealed.

"The Baron's a family man now, sir." The groom stamped his feet and tucked his hands under his armpits.

"What has that to do with anything?"

A handbill abandoned by some reveler from one of last night's fetes skimmed over the cobbles and spooked the other two horses, a charcoal gelding by the name of Poor Boy on account of the loss of his equine manhood; and a muscular dun. The groom had a dicey moment what with the cold having numbed his fingers but managed to send the sheet skittering to freedom.

"Man with a family can't leave anywhere spot on the dot," the groom said.

"I don't see why."

The door to number twenty-four flew open with a ringing crack of wood against stone. Of the two men who came out, the taller was Benjamin Dunbartin, Baron Aldreth, the owner of the house. He moved down the stairs at a rapid clip, clapping his hat onto his blond head as if he meant to cement it in place. The other man gripped his hat in one hand and descended at a more leisurely pace. The wind whipped a mass of inky curls over his sharp cheekbones.

"My lord." The groom handed Benjamin the reins to the dun. Before the groom could so much as offer a leg up, Ben launched himself into the saddle without a word of greeting or acknowledgment. Most everyone liked Benjamin. With his good looks and boyish smile, it was practically impossible not to. At the moment, however, Cynssyr thought Ben did not look like a man who cared for the family life.

"Come along, Devon," Benjamin said to his companion. He spoke with such force his dun tossed its head and pranced in nearly a full circle before Ben had him under control again.

Cynssyr's green eyes widened. "Have you quarreled with Mary?"

"Certainly not," said Ben.

"Well, you look like you've been hit by lightning from on high and still hear the angels singing. What's put you in such a state?"

"None of your damned business." The dun stamped hard on the cobbles, and Ben swore under his breath.

Cynssyr's bay snorted, and he reached to soothe the animal. "I should say it is, if I'm to endure such behavior from you."

"Devon!"

"Is this, by any chance, about Devon's letter?"

Ben's neck fairly snapped, he turned so quickly. "What do you know about that damned letter?"

"He wouldn't let me read it, but it must have succeeded. Camilla Fairchild is too young to be looking at a man that way." Cynssyr's mouth quirked and with the slight smile his austere features softened. When he smiled, he was about as handsome as a man could get, a fact not lost on him. He knew quite well the effect of his smile on the fairer sex.

Devon reached the curb in time to overhear the last remark. Coal-black eyes, at the moment completely without humor, slid from Ben to Cynssyr. "Disgraceful, ain't it? Her mother ought to set the girl a better example." He, too, accepted the reins of his gelding from the groom. He glanced at the stairs.

"Do you think she will?" Cynssyr managed, quite deliberately, to sound as though he hoped she wouldn't. Christ, he hoped not. He fully expected to soon discover what Mrs. Fairchild's backside felt like under his hands. Soft, he imagined. Energetic, he hoped.

"You ought to know better, Cyn," Devon said. "Even Mary said so."

"You will be relieved to know that at lord Sather's rout Miss Fairchild's passion was as yet untempered by experience. I merely provided her some." His smile reappeared. "A regrettably small amount, to be sure."

"You know, Cyn," Ben said, "one of these days you're going to miscalculate and find yourself married to some featherbrained female who'll bore you to tears."

"What else have you done, Devon, that's made him such wretched company?" Cynssyr kept one eye on Benjamin.

"Not one word," Ben said, glaring not at Cynssyr but at Devon.

Devon stopped with one foot in the stirrup to gift the world with affronted innocence. "All I did was—"

"Not one!" Ben turned a warning glance on him, too. "Not a word from you, either, Cyn."

Dev shook his head and mounted, exchanging a glance with Cynssyr who shrugged and found himself still mystified.

Only when the three were long out of earshot of the groom and riding toward Hyde Park did Ben speak. "How dare you?" He took a crumpled sheet of paper from his pocket and thrust it at Devon. "How dare you!"

"My personal correspondence is none of your affair." Devon, who had never expected to come into his title, could nevertheless exude more condescension than ever his father had managed, and the previous earl had been a master.

"Give me one reason I oughtn't call you out."

"Now see here," Cynssyr said, more than a little alarmed.

"Frankly, Cyn, if you knew about the letter, I ought to have satisfaction from you, too." Ben turned back to Devon. "Well?"

"I asked permission to court her when we were at Rosefeld for your wedding. But I had not the proper credentials then." Devon laughed bleakly. "I am Bracebridge now."

"Four years ago," Cynssyr said, "Camilla Fairchild was all of what, twelve or thirteen?"

"Good God," said Benjamin. "Not Miss Fairchild."

Devon snatched the crumpled paper from Ben's hand. "I won't lose her a second time."

"Lose whom?" Cynssyr drew even with Devon. "What are you two talking about? Devon, I thought your letter was for Miss Fairchild." Two women out for a morning walk stopped their stroll to stare at the men riding by. Out of pure habit, Cynssyr gave them an assessing glance, which made Devon laugh.

"Have you declared yourself?" Ben waved at the paper in Devon's hand. "Besides in that note of yours, I mean."

"If not Miss Fairchild, then whom?" Cynssyr said, by now more than a little annoyed. "Miss George?" When that got no reply, he said, "Not Miss Willowby. Oh, please, no. If it's Miss Willowby, I forbid it."

Devon slid the note into his pocket. "She has not the slightest idea of my feelings."

"Good God."

"Now that she is here in London," Devon said, "I mean to change that." He pulled back on his black, waiting for Ben's dun to draw alongside. Once again, Cynssyr found himself maddeningly excluded. "With your permission, of course."

"It isn't my permission you need be concerned with," Ben said. "It's her father's."

"The old man can bugger himself for all I care." The black-as-the-depths-of-hell eyes that even Cynssyr, who knew better, sometimes thought devoid of life flashed with a violent fire.

Benjamin grinned.

They were at the Park now, off the streets and onto the riding paths. "Would one of you," said Cynssyr, "please tell me what the devil you're talking about?"

"Dev thinks he's in love."

"That much I gathered." He looked over at Devon. "In love with whom?"

"My sister-in-law," Ben said, throwing up one hand. "That's who."

Cynssyr gave Devon a look. "Which one?" He moved out of the path of a fat gentleman on a white mare. To the best of his recollection, there were four Sinclair sisters and Benjamin had married one of them. That left three. And, if memory served, the Sinclair sisters deserved their reputation for beauty. Ben's wife, Mary, was among the most beautiful women of Cynssyr's rather vast acquaintance. He almost didn't blame Ben for marrying her.

"I don't *think* I'm in love."

"The youngest? Miss Emily?" His green eyes flickered with interest. "If she turns out half as beautiful as she promised, she'll cause a riot at her debut."

"No. And stay the hell away from Emily, Cyn."

"Then it must be the brunette. Lucy." The name rolled off his tongue replete with his recollection of ebony hair and features of heartbreaking perfection.

"No."

"You mean the eldest?" He could not for the life of him summon an image of the eldest Sinclair sister. "That's impossible. I don't even remember her."

"Blonde? Gray-blue eyes. Yay tall." Ben indicated an inch or so below his chin which meant a tall woman, perhaps even an ungainly one. "You'll meet her tonight at the ball. Meet her again, that is."

"Why don't I recall her?" Cynssyr glanced at Devon.

"And by the way," Ben said. "Stay away from Lucy, too."

"Why?"

"Because when it comes to women, damn you, Cynssyr, you're a rogue, that's why."

"Mama begins to despair. Perhaps I ought put to rest her doubts of a succession."

Ben snorted. "I'd not curse any of my sisters-in-law with you for a husband."

"Now that," Cynssyr said, "wounds me deeply. When at last I marry, I expect I'll make a most excellent husband."

"Hah," said Devon.

"*Et tu, Bruté?*"

"You can't even settle on what woman to seduce tonight."

"If not for Napoleon, I'd likely be years married. A positive dullard, like Ben here." But Napoleon there was, so Cynssyr wasn't married at all. Love, naturally, would have but a limited role in any marriage he contracted. The war had burned out his capacity, if ever he'd possessed it, for such saving emotion.

"A dullard?" said Ben, spoiling his attempt to appear insulted by breaking into laughter. Devon rolled his eyes.

"Whatever you two think, I'm quite aware I need a wife. A man of my station requires a wife, as my desperate mother so often reminds me."

"God help the woman fool enough to marry you," Ben said.

"Why not one of your sisters-in-law, Ben? It seems an excellent idea." Dozens of suitable candidates were thrown his way every season, this one being no different from any other since the war. But he'd not been able to bring himself to the sticking point with any of them.

"No."

"I'll reform." He grinned. "I promise."

"You'll reform when hell freezes over."

A faint memory tickled at the back of his mind. He tapped his temple. "You mean the spinster, don't you, Devon? The eldest. The one with the spectacles."

"Blond hair, gray-blue eyes. Yay tall," Benjamin repeated.

"What was her name?"

Ben's blue eyes chilled another degree. "Anne."

"Gad. I still don't remember her. Except for the spectacles." He looked askance at Dev. "I have never understood his taste in women."

"You truly want to marry Anne?" Ben asked Devon. Curiosity and relief lingered at the edges of the question, but hearing him, no one could doubt the seriousness of the matter. No doting father could have sounded more cautious.

"Yes."

"I meant to introduce her to Declan McHenry," said Ben, looking thoughtfully at Devon. "Or Phillip Lovejoy."

"I'd be obliged if you didn't."

"Good God, you are serious, aren't you?"

"It's been four years. I am done waiting." Amusement brightened Devon's brooding eyes and made his severe mouth curve in a surprisingly warm smile. It did interesting things to his face, the way severity gave way to warmth. At times like this, when he saw Devon smile, Cynssyr understood exactly why women went so eagerly to his bed.

If Devon had really decided the Sinclair spinster was the woman he wanted, then the matter was done. He would have his way. The why of it mystified him. Even as plain Devon Carlisle, he could do far better than some dried-up female who wasn't even pretty enough to bother taking off her spectacles. As matrimonial material, the earl of Bracebridge was nearly as sought after as he himself. Nearly. But, not quite.

"Enough. No more blather about love and marriage, you two," Cynssyr said. With a flick of the reins, he steered his horse past a fallen branch then cantered to the edge of a meadow where he waited for Ben and Devon.

"Jade," Ben accused when he reached the meadow.

Cynssyr flashed a brilliantly arrogant smile. "The trouble with you, my lord Baron Aldreth, is you love your wife. And you, Devon. For shame. You disappoint me. You disappoint all our sex, falling for this Miss Sinclair."

"Love," said Dev with one of his wry grins. "A most heinous crime."

"Love." Cynssyr lifted one brow in the supercilious disdain he usually reserved for certain rebuttals in the Lords. "You mean a man's delusion he's not been robbed of his freedom and a woman's that she's gained hers?"

"Exactly," Devon said.

"How can you trust your judgment now?" He lifted his riding whip, but brought it down on his boot leg, not his horse. "Fools the both of you." So saying, he urged his horse to a gallop. "Anne Sinclair," he muttered. He heard Devon and Ben thunder after him and gave his horse its head. They had no chance of catching him now. Only the best horseflesh found its way into his stables. He had the best of everything. Wine. Horses. Women. Friends.

He wanted to roar with disgust and dismay. Devon married. What was he to do with himself then? To the devil with spinsters who set their caps on marriage, he thought as the chill wind whipped past him. "To the very devil with her." Thus did the duke of Cynssyr, so deservedly referred to as Lord Ruin, dismiss the woman with whom he would soon be desperately in love.

INDISCREET

CHAPTER 1

Lord Edward Marrack refused more wine when the bottle came around in his direction. Instead, he leaned against his chair while his friend the Earl of Crosshaven raised a hand—Cross was inevitably the center of attention—and said, with significant stress, the two words, "Sabine Godard."

The other men in the room looked impressed. No one, including Lord Edward, doubted for a moment that Cross had indeed secured the person of Miss Sabine Godard.

Up to now, the young lady's reputation had been unassailable. She was an orphan who had been raised by her uncle since she was quite young. They made their home in Oxford, the city of spires, Henry Godard having been a don there and a noted philosopher until his recent retirement from those hallowed walls. She and her uncle had come to London so that Godard could receive a knighthood in recognition of his intellectual contributions to king and empire.

They had not been long in London, the Godards, but Lord Edward recalled hearing Miss Godard was reckoned a pretty girl. Very pretty and quite unavailable. She was, if he had his facts in order, her uncle's permanent caretaker, as was often the fate of children not raised by their parents. Her uncle was now Sir Henry Godard. By several large steps, quite a come up in the world for them both.

The unavailable Miss Godard had been pursued by Crosshaven. That, too, Lord Edward had heard. The Earl of Crosshaven was angelically, devilishly, beautiful. His manners were exquisite and his intellect absolutely first-rate. Lord Edward would not bother with a friendship if that were not the case. But Crosshaven, in Lord Edward's opinion, was not as familiar with discretion as he might be. Something he was proving tonight.

Though Lord Edward liked Cross exceedingly, this boast of his was infamous. Ungentlemanly, in fact. That Cross had refilled his glass far too often in the course of the evening was no excuse for his revealing to anyone that he had seduced a young woman of decent family. And, one presumed, abandoned her to whatever fate her uncle might decide was fit for a girl who strayed from what was proper.

"How was she?" asked one of the other young bucks.

Cross kissed the tips of his fingers and arced his thus blessed hand toward the ceiling. That engendered several ribald comments, some having to do with Cross's prowess in the bedroom and others having to do with Sabine Godard and what Crosshaven may or may not have taught her about sexual congress and how to fornicate with élan.

In Lord Edward's opinion, Cross, though just short of thirty, and for all his lofty titles, had now proved he had a great deal to learn about honor and decency. This evening, which had begun as a pleasant interlude with men he liked, no longer seemed very pleasant.

"A seduction," Lord Edward said to no one in particular, "when properly carried out, pleases both parties for the duration, while a break humiliates no one."

"Who says I've broken with her?" Crosshaven asked.

"I do," he replied. "And any fool with half a brain."

Crosshaven shook his head sadly. "Is this what happens to a man when he falls in love? If I didn't know better, I'd accuse you of not wanting to go to bed with a pretty young woman." He winked. "Without benefit of marriage, I mean." He gave Lord Edward a sloppy smile, then looked around the room with his glass held high in a mock toast. "To Sabine Godard."

"Hear, hear," said a few of the others. Most just took the opportunity to sample their wine.

Crosshaven took another drink of his hock, but he kept his eyes on Lord Edward as he did. He'd noticed Lord Edward hadn't joined in the toast. "Don't be such a bloody bore, Ned," he said with a roll of his eyes. "You're not married yet, old man."

"True." But in three months time he would be. God, he was weary of this, of nights like this spent drinking or whoring and living as if there weren't something more to be had from life. He wasn't married yet, but wished Rosaline was already his wife.

Lord Edward put down his glass and stood. He felt a giant. With reason. He towered over everyone in the room, standing or not. "Good evening, gentlemen, my lords."

"What?" said Cross. He was a bit unsteady on his feet. "Are you leaving already, Ned? It's early yet."

Lord Edward could not bring himself to smile to soften his disapproval of his friend's behavior. Nor could he remain silent. "I do not care to hear any lady's character shredded for the sake of a man's reputation."

Cross focused on Lord Edward, registered the slight to his honor, and said, "She's no better than she ought to be."

"True," Lord Edward said. "But the consequences of indiscretion always fall hardest on the woman. Tonight, you are lauded for your seduction of the girl, deemed ever more manly. Your reputation as a cocksman is firmly established."

Crosshaven bowed amid a few catcalls. He straightened, grinning. Lord Edward was probably the only one in the room who wasn't grinning back.

"What reason had you to prove that fact at the cost of her reputation? No one disputes your appeal to the fairer sex." Lord Edward sighed. There was no point in lecturing Cross. No point at all "Tomorrow," he said with regret soft in his voice, "Miss Godard will not find the world so pleasant a. place. That is a fate you ought to have avoided for the girl."

"She's still no better than she ought to be, Ned." He pretended to sober up, but as a drunk would do. Sloppily. "I mean no disrespect, Lord Edward. But it's true about the girl. No better than she ought to be."

He acknowledged Cross with a nod, without smiling because he was disappointed in his friend. "Nor are you."

As he walked out, Lord Edward thought it was a very great pity that Miss Godard was so thoroughly ruined. Beyond repair. Crosshaven's boast of her would be everywhere by noon tomorrow. He did not know the girl person-ally but did not like to think of the disgrace that was soon to fall on her and her uncle. They would both be touched by Crosshaven's indiscretion.

He thought it likely the newly knighted Sir Henry Godard would put her onto the street.

CHAPTER 2

One year and eight months later, give or take a few days.
May 5, 1811

> The former Lord Edward Marrack was now the Marquess of Foye and a guest at the palace of an English merchant in Buyukdere, Turkey, about twelve miles outside Constantinople. Europeans were not permitted to live in the city, and Buyukdere was a favorite summer residence for expatriates from any number of countries. Including England. A good deal of the diplomatic corps resided in Buyukdere, which overlooked the blue, blue waters of the Bosporus.

THE FINEST WOMAN here tonight was Miss Sabine Godard.

How strange that he should cross paths with Miss Godard so many thousands of miles from home. Foye wasn't surprised to find she was a lovely woman.

If Crosshaven had noticed her, and, quite infamously, he had, it stood to reason she would have something. She did.

Foye sat on a chair not so far from the center of the assembly that he would be thought aloof, though he'd been accused of that and worse since he'd begun his tour of countries that had the single advantage of being far from England. He was not by nature a gregarious man and was even less so now, or so he'd been told by people who had known him before—True enough. For the second time in his life, he was a changed man. What a pity he didn't like the change.

Now that he saw her before him, he understood why so many men had spoken of her looks and why Crosshaven had chosen her, it wasn't so much that she was beautiful. She wasn't quite that. A man didn't catch his breath at the sight of her. She was not a very tall woman, though from what he could see of her, her figure was a nice one. He stared at her, trying to pin down for himself the reason that she was a more attractive woman than she ought to be.

Her features were too strong for beauty in the classic sense, though anyone meeting her for the first time would think her pretty. She smiled often, and he'd watched several men stare, besotted, when her mouth curved a certain way. Her hair was an astonishing shade of gold. Curls at her temples and brow gave her an air of sweetness without being cloying, and there weren't many pretty young women who could manage that. A lace cap was on her head, a jade green ribbon threaded through the material. She wasn't beautiful, no, not that, but she was pretty. Exceptionally so.

She had something else as well, and he was determined to put a name to whatever elusive quality that was. What a shame Crosshaven had ruined everything for her. She might have done well for herself, had she stayed in London. There were any number of pretty young girls who'd married up. Some decent young man would likely have thought himself lucky to marry a woman like her. Foye couldn't help feeling at least partially responsible for the fact that she hadn't.

At the moment. Miss Godard was sitting at a table surrounded by men in uniform; sailors, soldiers of the Royal Artillery, Royal Engineers, or otherwise attached to the military here in Buyukdere. She was reading tea leaves for them and having a grand time, too. Despite her smiles, and despite the men gathered around her, she appeared unaware of the flirtatious looks and remarks sent her way, but not, he thought, unaware of her looks.

Miss Godard knew very well that men found her attractive, Foye decided. But she was not a flirt.

Her uncle, Sir Henry Godard, sat close enough to her that she could easily lean over and touch his arm should she care to. Sir Henry was deep in conversation with one of the merchants who worked for the Levant Company. The topic at hand, from what Foye could overhear, was the merits and demerits of St. Augustine. A heady subject for afternoon tea.

So far, Sir Henry had the advantage in the argument. He was a wily debater. Leading his prey to make admissions that seemed reasonable enough while, in reality, he was laying a trap such that when it sprang his victim would have no choice but to cede Sir Henry's entire point.

Experience had etched deep lines in Sir Henry's face and yet had taken a disproportionate physical toll on the rest of his body. His upper back was hunched, throwing his leonine head forward. His hair was that off shade of white, a yellowish silver, common to men who'd been blond throughout their adult lives. Notwithstanding the depredations of age and illness, Sir Henry was a man of considerable presence. His profession remained in his manner of speech, his temperament and even his gestures. It was easy to imagine him addressing a lecture hall of young men and terrifying them into listening at peril of their very survival.

The salon was filled with guests holding teacups and guarding plates of cakes, biscuits, and sugar wafers. There were tables piled with watermelon and bowls of sherbet in silver cups with delicate silver spoons. The merchant whose palace this was, Mr. Anthony Lucey, had invited only Englishmen and women this afternoon, though naturally men outnumbered the women, who were, for the most part wives or other relatives of the soldiers. Some of the men were employees of the Levant Company who had raised families here. A pretty English girl wasn't unheard of in Buyukdere. Not by any means.

Lucey himself, a longtime friend of Foye's late father, stood in the center of the room telling a story Foye had heard before about the time he'd gotten lost in Mayfair and had mistakenly knocked on the Duke of Portland's private door. Lucey was such an excellent raconteur the tale still amused more than forty years after it had happened.

He was beginning to think, though, that he ought to go get himself introduced to Miss Godard. Just to see what she was like. Naturally, he was curious. And since he was here, if the circumstances offered, he might explain what had happened.

Foye resisted the urge to smooth down his hair. There really was no dealing with his curls. They were contrary by innate disposition, it seemed. A good match for his face, which was one of the reasons he'd let his hair grow and never cut it short again. With a face that defined "ill made" and a body that tended to intimidate by sheer size—he had always been prone to muscle—Foye was used to women looking past him or away from him. Though since he'd become Foye, that happened marginally less often.

He plucked a crisp sugar wafer from his plate and took a bite. A touch of almond, he thought, and he had a taste of bliss melting over his tongue. Lucey's cook was superb, a Neapolitan man he'd succeeded in hiring away from the Italian ambassador's residence. The story of Lucey's raid on the Italian kitchen was amusing, too. Foye took another bite of his wafer and savored it while he watched yet another lovesick young officer beg to have his fortune told by Miss Godard.

Perhaps, he thought, it was something about the way she looked at a man. Yes. Something about her eyes. And her complete disinterest. What bold young man didn't want the very woman who wouldn't have him? Given all that he and Miss Godard had in common, he ought to at least meet her. It was, however, quite plain to him that to get anywhere with the niece one must start with the uncle.

When Foye was done eating, he asked Lucey for an introduction to Sir Henry.

The old man was formidable; that had been apparent even from a distance. Closer up, he seemed no less so for all that his frailness was the more evident. He had, Foye recalled, read one of Sir Henry's treatises, the 1805 *On Hubris*.

When Lucey walked him over to the philosopher, Foye was speared by a pair of iron gray eyes that would have been at home in a man forty years his junior, they were that bright and perceptive. He did not believe it was an accident that he should think back on his university days with some sense of dread. This man would have had no compunction whatever about sending a prince packing for want of preparation. No more a mere second son—all that Foye had been in those days.

Foye bowed when Lucey completed the introduction. Already the object of much curiosity on account of his appearance, more stares came his way when his titles were pronounced. Lucey, unfortunately, knew the entire list. Marquess of Foye. Earls of Eidenderry and DeMortmercy. He was used to them now, at last accustomed to the change in his identity from Lord Edward to Foye. There were days now when he could hardly recall a time when he hadn't been Foye. His first titled ancestor had been ennobled before the reign of Charlemagne. The Marracks of Cornwall had never been viscounts. Their nobility had begun with an earldom.

It was with him that the Marrack line would end. With the death of his brother without any living children, he was the last of the Marrack men. When he died, his properties and titles would revert to the crown. What a failure to take to his grave, to leave no one to carry on the name.

"Well, well, young man," Sir Henry said, laboriously craning his neck sideways to look at him. "That is a mouthful of names."

Foye smiled despite himself. He had not been called a young man for a good many years. It wasn't as though he was old, but at thirty-eight, he wasn't a boy anymore. Godard held out a gnarled hand for Foye to take, which he did, gently. The philosopher was crippled with the gout, and his skin was hot to the touch.

"Yes, Sir Henry, it is, indeed, a mouthful." He smiled, aware of Miss Godard's attention to their exchange. Would he tell her, if the opportunity arose? He ought to but didn't know if he would. She seemed to have made a life for herself here, far from England. Why bring up what could only be painful memories for her? Because, Foye thought, if he were her, he'd want to know the truth. "I hope you were not bored listening to all that."

"Not at all." Sir Henry bobbed his head. "I am pleased to make your acquaintance, my Lord Foye."

"The pleasure is mine, Sir Henry." Foye was aware that Miss Godard had stopped her inspection of someone's teacup—what nonsense that business was—to listen to the introduction.

Did she recognize his name from his connection with Crosshaven? Perhaps she did not know he and Cross had been friends and that Foye knew what had been done to her. Or perhaps she did, and now wondered if her reputation was to be ruined again by someone else who knew only the lies.

"Foye. Foye," Sir Henry said, tapping his chin with a finger permanently hooked into a claw. He narrowed his eyes and gave him a sideways look. "A King's College man, weren't you?"

Foye bowed. For a split second, he racked his brain for the essay he must have failed to write. "Yes, sir."

"Your elder brother, too, if I'm not mistaken."

"You are not."

"I thought so." Sir Henry grinned and nodded. "You were Lord Edward then, not Foye. That's why I didn't know who you were until you were close enough for me to see you." He pulled at a blanket spread over his lap. "Took a first in mathematics, didn't you?"

"I'm astonished you should know such a thing." It was at university that Foye had learned there were women who cared more for what he offered when they were intimate than for what he looked like in broad daylight. He'd also discovered he had a talent for pleasing his partners. He'd made himself an assiduous student of the delights to be had between a man and woman. Well.

No more of that for him. Those days were long gone. He was done with that life.

Godard waved a misshapen hand. "I made it a point to acquaint myself with the names of all the young men of promise. If we were at home, I would send Sabine to find my entry on you." He smiled, and the effect was disconcertingly sly. His niece looked in their direction at the mention of her name. "I kept a ledger, my lord. I followed you in Parliament, you know. Heard your maiden speech. I am rarely wrong in my predictions."

"Am I to be flattered by that?" Foye asked. He did not look at Miss Godard, though he burned to do so.

"I should think so. I saw you once or twice at university." He chuckled. "No mistaking you for anyone else."

He smiled again. "No, sir."

"I should think you learned early on it's better to have something here"—he tapped his temple—"than to have a handsome face. Too many young men these days spend hours primping at the mirror when they would profit more from improving their minds."

"Godard," his niece murmured. She put an arm on her uncle's sleeve in a gesture familiar enough to be habitual. Foye could easily imagine her needing to restrain her uncle's bluntness. For all Sir Henry's rudeness, he rather liked the man for it. He wasn't a pretty man, after all.

"What?" Sir Henry said, turning his torso toward his niece. "With a face like his, do you think he bothers much with enriching his tailor over his bookseller?"

"I think Lord Foye is very smartly dressed," she said.

"Thank you," Foye said. In point of fact, he was vain of his appearance. Even as Lord Edward, he had never walked out of his house without clothes that made other men beg him for the name of his tailor.

"Look at him." One thin arm shot into the air. "Do you think he spent his time at King's with his mistresses instead of in the library?"

Good God. Foye held back his shock at Sir Henry's speech. Miss Godard, too, felt the indiscretion, for her cheeks pinked up. Sir Henry didn't seem to think anything of his declaration.

"Godard." She slid a glance at Foye, and their eyes met. Hers were brown. There was nothing extraordinary about her eyes, but for the intelligence there. She was no ordinary girl, he thought. "Forgive him," she murmured.

"For what?" Foye said. "It's true. I am no model of masculine beauty. I am not offended by Sir Henry pointing that out." Age had its privileges, after all; and Sir Henry had to be nearer seventy than sixty. He had decided to be amused. There was brilliance yet in the old man.

"Sensible of you, my boy."

Foye nodded to Sir Henry, but he was absorbed by Miss Godard. She was a far more interesting woman than he'd expected. All this time, whenever he thought of Crosshaven and what he'd done that night, he'd been imagining a sweet young woman, weeping for her lost reputation. Naive and mourning the infamous wrong done her. Miss Godard was hardly naive.

"Have you been in Anatolia long, my lord?" Sir Henry said.

"No," Foye replied.

Miss Godard was now indisputably a part of their conversation. He could not help but look at her. Her eyes were not a common brown after all, but something a more poetic man might call dark honey. From the shape of her mouth, the tilt of her eyes with their thick, dark lashes, to the sweeping line of her throat to her shoulders, she was the sort of woman who made a man think of darkened rooms and whispered endearments. He understood very well why Crosshaven had chosen her.

"I arrived in Constantinople yesterday," Foye said to Sir Henry. "And you?"

Sir Henry folded his crippled hands on his lap. "We have been in Buyukdere coming onto a month. Is that correct, Sabine?"

She answered without hesitation. "In Anatolia, forty-three days. In Buyukdere, twenty-one, Uncle."

Again, Foye felt his understanding of Miss Godard to be maddeningly incomplete. Not a woman wronged and mourning her fate. Not a pretty girl who knew and used the power her looks gave her over a man. And to speak so crisply, with such unhesitating precision. He preferred it when the people he met fell into neat categories. Irascible old man. A young woman wronged. Foye did not yet know where to fit Miss Godard.

"Twenty-one days, my lord," Sir Henry told him with a smile that conveyed his pride in the precision of his niece's recollection.

The naval officer whose tea leaves she'd been reading bid Miss Godard adieu. She nodded, said good-bye, and though the officer waited for her to say something more, she didn't. For the moment, her table was empty of a companion, yet all the other men who had been waiting for their chance found themselves dismissed without a word.

"You have an able assistant, sir." There was an awkward silence during which Foye expected to be introduced and was not. He cleared his throat and returned a bit of the older man's directness. "May I meet your niece, Sir Henry?"

"What for?" Sir Henry's eyes scalded. Foye could only thank the Lord he'd never been in one of Sir Henry's lectures when he was at Oxford. He would have quailed under that gimlet eye. Because, in truth, he had spent more time with his various mistresses than with his studies.

"Godard," Miss Godard said, firmly this time.

Sir Henry tipped his head toward her. "Very well. I suppose there's no hope for it. Sabine, will you meet the Marquess of Foye?"

She stood to curtsey but did not extend a hand to him over the very small table at which she sat. He bowed in return. "Delighted to make your acquaintance, my lord."

"My niece, sir. Miss Sabine Godard."

"Miss Godard." He was aware he was staring too hard. She was still so very young. He doubted she was much beyond twenty. Crosshaven ought to rot in hell for what he'd done to the girl.

She cocked her head at him, and at that moment he would have given anything to know what she was thinking.

"Would you read my future?" he asked.

Sir Henry snorted. "It's nonsense, my lord," he said. "She knows that, too."

Miss Godard's gaze flicked to her uncle; she remained unruffled. "If he is on your list of men who will make something of themselves, Godard, I daresay he is well aware my tea reading is a nothing more than an amusing way to pass the time." She turned to him. "My lord, have you a cup you've been drinking? If not, you'll need fresh."

He pointed in the direction of the table on which he'd set his tea. "There."

"That should do." She smiled at him, but with no particular interest in him beyond what was polite and no indication that she cared anything for his title or his consequence. Or his lack of beauty, for that matter. How egalitarian of her. "I'll wait, my lord."

He returned with his nearly empty cup and sat on the chair opposite her. His legs were too long to fit underneath the table, leaving him no choice but to sit sideways or remain as he was with his thighs wide open. He turned on the chair. Miss Godard took his cup and looked into it. "Can you bear to drink another mouthful or two?"

He nodded. He would tell her, he decided. He would tell her about Crosshaven and then apologize for his role in her ruin, limited as it had been. He took back his cup, drank it nearly empty, and extended it to her.

"No," she said, refusing his cup. "Hold it just so and swirl the contents thus." She demonstrated the desired motion with her arm.

"Nonsense, all of it," Sir Henry said.

"Yes, Godard," she said without looking at her uncle. But he saw a smile lurking on her mouth. "Excellent. Now upend your cup on the saucer."

"Shall I first cross your palms with silver?" Foye asked.

"Certainly not." Her eyes, her very fine eyes, flashed with humor. There was more to Miss Godard than she meant to let on, he realized. "If I allowed you to pay me in order to learn your future, my ability to accurately assess what tomorrow and beyond may hold for you would be compromised."

"Consider the offer rescinded, miss."

Her mouth quirked. "Anyone who takes filthy lucre is no better than a rank charlatan."

Obediently, he swirled his cup and did as directed, upending the cup over the saucer. Though he did not like to admit it, she interested him. What was she? What had she become since Crosshaven? "And you, being above remuneration, are no charlatan, I presume?"

Her smile became a direct and knowing connection with his gaze. "I am the worst charlatan in Christendom if you believe a word I say, my lord." She righted his tea and stared into it. "This is utter nonsense, as you well know."

"My future?" He sighed. "I feared as much."

Miss Godard laughed softly. "Divination, my lord. As much as I admire the great civilizations of the past, I have concluded there is a reason men of modern learning do not maintain a belief in the ancient ways. Just as there were no gods on Mount Olympus, there is no magic by which one can infer the future from random patterns made in tea leaves." She quirked her eyebrows at him. "Or the entrails of a goat, for that matter."

He very nearly laughed. Nearly. My God, she was quick witted and not afraid to show him. "Nevertheless, this"—he indicated the teacup—"is, as you say, quite a charming pastime for a lady to have."

"Thank you." She raised her voice. "You see, Godard, that I am vindicated by Lord Foye."

"What's that?" Sir Henry said.

"The marquess finds the reading of tea leaves to be an amusing occupation." She spoke so drolly and with such affection for her uncle that Foye was hard-pressed not to grin. Miss Godard handled her irascible uncle quite well.

"More the fool he," Sir Henry said.

Miss Godard lifted a hand and pressed the other to her upper bosom. "A moment of silence while I read the portents, my lord."

She could have been an actress; the gesture and tone of voice were so perfectly done. No wonder the officers vied for her attention. For one thing, she was miserly with it, and when she did look at you directly, there was so much there to see in her eyes, a man could not be faulted for wanting more. He leaned his side against his chair, his elbow over the back, and stretched out one leg while he watched her. "I believe," he said in a low voice, "that we have a mutual acquaintance."

Without taking her eyes from his cup, she replied in a soft voice, "Not a mutual friend, I am afraid. Unless you mean someone besides the Earl of Crosshaven."

"I do not."

Her expression closed off. "You have a bouquet of flowers, here." She pointed to a mass of leaves. "That signifies you are to be happy in love."

"I was," he said. "Once. But no longer."

She looked at him. "I am not reading your past, my lord, but your future."

"Happy in love?" he said, looking into her eyes. "I fear that is quite impossible."

"The tea leaves never lie," she replied.

He wriggled his fingers over his cup. "Pray continue."

Made in the USA
Coppell, TX
13 December 2022